MIGRATION

A COSMO BENNETT MAPPING NOVELLA

J.A. JERNAY

PLOTWORKS PUBLISHING

ISBN (electronic): 978-1-960936-31-8

ISBN (print): 978-1-960936-32-5

AUTHOR'S NOTE

The island of Tatuaga exists only in our imagination. However, the experience of its people does represent the experience of many Eastern Caribbean peoples.

CHAPTER
ONE

THE ISLAND OF TATUAGA, EASTERN ANTILLES, CARIBBEAN

His family back home called him Bulge. A single glance at the man explained the nickname. There were piles of muscles on nearly every part of his body. They weren't finely delineated aesthetic gym muscles, either. They were functional muscles, which meant sheer mass with little definition. It never looks as strong as it really is, not unless you know better, and sometimes you only know better after finding yourself on the wrong end of it. Bulge had earned this strength by hauling boats, carrying ropes, cutting stone, and rolling oil tanks with his brothers, sister, father, and others.

On the back of his neck, in a neat line from left to right, was a tattoo. Three words.

Diamants sont éternels.

Bulge was as hard as a stone. That's why his family had relied on him far more than they did on his brother and sister. That's also why they'd sent him here, to Tatuaga, with a very specific goal. Bulge had only come to this island twice in his life—his family rarely traveled off their home island—so it had taken him nearly a week to learn the roads, watch the comings and goings.

But eventually he'd found the target.

This morning, he had settled down in a café on Worthington Road, which was about a mile and a half long. It led from a local neighborhood, up in the mountains on the outskirts of town, to the main tourist zone downtown at the water's edge. This café was closer to the tourist end, where he might stand out a little less, though Bulge never really blended in anywhere.

This vantage point afforded him the perfect view of the local families walking down the hill into town. The tuk-tuks would bring them back up later, at least the ones who could afford it. But the view from here was stunning. The one-lane dirt road hugged the side of the mountain, tall red-and-yellow tropical flowers sprouting out of the green crevices on the sides. Far below, the deep azure of the Caribbean waters spread out like a blue shag carpet.

The café itself was a repurposed shotgun shack. Some enterprising soul had gentrified it, presumably the thin woman inside who owned the place. She'd mounted a sign in French script, written a small menu in white chalk on a black slate, and placed four tiny iron tables on the patio outside.

Bulge sat delicately behind one of them, a small espresso untouched before him on the yellow tiled tabletop. A pair of wraparound sunglasses perched on his huge bald skull, and his full lips were calm and purposeful. His small, narrow nose betrayed almost nothing beyond an occasional twitch. His large brown hands rested calmly on the tops of his thighs like a pair of sleeping attack dogs.

He was watching for the boy.

The locals came shuffling down the road past the café.

Some were clad in t-shirts and shorts and sandals, others in white collar shirts and black pants and shoes, on their way to their service jobs at one of the resorts. Tatuaga had found new life as a tourist destination in the last two decades.

Bulge reached into his light blue fanny pack. He'd worn it on purpose, to fit in with the tourist hordes. It also provided a convenient way to carry the necessary tools for achieving his goal. From the side zip pocket, he removed a photo and placed it on the table next to his coffee. He covered most of the photo with a napkin, just enough to let him see the target.

The boy in the photo looked to be about twelve years old. He was brown too, with a round face and a crooked smile. His gangly limbs hung loosely from his body. Over his shoulder was slung a bright red backpack. The boy wasn't unusual. Just a normal kid, with a long life in his future.

He'd have that life too, if he didn't give any trouble.

Using a paper napkin, Bulge patted the sweat off his upper lip. Behind the wraparound sunglasses, his eyes scanned the locals as they strolled by. So far the only children who'd passed by were either toddlers or elementary school age.

He checked the fanny pack one more time. Inside was a switchblade knife that he'd purchased new at a tourist shop, plus a backup that he'd brought over in his bag. There was pepper spray, which he'd smuggled into the country as well. And there was the RFID smart card that would get him back into the port of Tatuaga, where the boat awaited his signal.

"Can I get you anything else?" said a voice.

He looked up. It was the thin woman, her long braids coiled on top of her head. A lengthy scar ran down one

3

forearm. For a moment, he wondered how that had happened.

"No, thanks," he said.

"Are you waiting for somebody?" Her eyes flicked down at the covered photo.

He shook his head no. "I'll take the bill."

"You sound like you from around here."

"I'm just visiting."

"Which resort are you staying at?"

His tone grew curt. "You get paid for all the questions, *maco*?"

The owner made a small harumph and went inside. Bulge resumed scanning the passersby.

There.

The boy was coming down the road. He was wearing an oversized white t-shirt, long gray shorts, and blue plastic sandals. His limbs bounced all over as though electrified. The red backpack was strapped securely to his back, the loops through both arms. Bulge's nose twitched. That made things more difficult.

However, the last three days, he'd come down with his mother. Bulge had made plans for that. Today, the boy was alone. That made the job easier.

When the boy passed the café, Bulge pulled out his phone. His large thumbs typed out a brief message. Ah go do it brah.

He pressed send, then stuffed the photo back in his fanny pack. He stood up and left the patio and followed the boy down the road. The thin owner of the café came out with the bill and shouted after him. Bulge ignored her.

The boy wandered down to the tourist zone. The crowds were light, it being off season and early in the morning. Bulge followed at a close distance. When the boy stopped to buy a fritter, Bulge paused to examine a rack of ceramic figurines in a window.

Up ahead was the small side street, Coach Lane, that Bulge had already targeted for the task. There was a bend, so a short stroll would provide cover from most eyes on the main road. It also offered a more-or-less direct path down to the docks, a quick four-minute walk away. He'd already timed it.

As the boy reached Coach Lane, Bulge cupped his hands to his mouth and shouted.

"Hey there boy!"

The kid turned around. Bulge walked towards him, his large pectorals pressing against his t-shirt.

"What?" the boy said.

Bulge held out his own phone. "You dropped this."

"No, I didn't."

"I saw you drop it! Don't play that game with me boy! This your phone!"

The boy munched on his fritter, his large white eyes flicking between the rectangular screen and Bulge's face.

"I know this belongs to you," said Bulge. "You want to see how I know?"

"How?"

"Come and follow me," said Bulge, "right down here. I'll show you."

He put his large hand on the boy's back and firmly guided him about fifteen paces down the road, staying to the inside part of the curve. The boy didn't resist. Old stone walls the height of a man ran both sides of the street here. The only business was a single roti takeaway shop, which would be closed until eleven am.

"Look," he said, holding up the screen, "I have a video right here that shows me that you are the owner of this phone."

The boy's eyes weren't on the screen. They were looking back at the main road. He was worried.

It was time.

Now.

In one swift movement, Bulge grabbed the boy's shoulders with both hands and spun him around. His left hand powerfully pinched the boy's neck and he pushed the small frame up against the stone wall. The boy's face was crushed sideways against the stone.

The boy began twisting and writhing instantly. He had good reaction time, but Bulge enjoyed first-mover advantage.

Then the boy began to scream. Bulge was expecting it. He pulled the child off the wall and clapped his right hand over his mouth. Two small feet danced uselessly on the cobblestones.

Bulge leaned down and said into the boy's ear. "Cooperate with me. I want your backpack."

The boy violently shook his head left and right. The word no tried to escape his throat. He was spirited.

Bulge shifted position, replanting his feet and putting the boy into a full headlock with his left arm. The boy struggled, so he squeezed harder. With his free right hand, Bulge unzipped his fanny pack and removed the switchblade. He flicked it open and held the point at the boy's face.

"I want what's in your bag."

He slipped the edge of the knife under the shoulder strap of the backpack and began to saw away at it. The boy tried to scream again. Bulge flexed harder, cutting off the boy's air, and the sound stopped.

Then something sharp slashed into Bulge's right leg. He grunted in surprise and dropped the switchblade. The boy's right hand had reached into his fanny pack and found Bulge's backup knife—a much more significant blade, three inches long and quite fat. He was swinging it around, trying to find Bulge's leg.

Bulge grabbed the boy's right hand with his right hand. His own dwarfed the boy's fist, encircling it easily. The kid's fingers were tight upon the handle with the terrified grip. He wasn't letting go of it.

Scowling, Bulge guided the knife up the twelve-year-old's body. Then he slashed the tip diagonally across the boy's chest. A red ribbon of blood appeared on the white t-shirt.

The boy crumpled in his arms.

The remainder of the job went quickly. Bulge easily pulled the backpack off the boy's shoulders and down his arms. The boy was in shock and didn't resist. When the backpack was finally free, Bulge dropped the boy's body to the ground.

"Hey!" a man's voice shouted. "What the hell do you think you're doing?"

It was a white American tourist, a man in his fifties, wearing a polo shirt and leather sandals. Unlike most, this one looked to be in decent shape. He was moving briskly down Coach Lane, towards Bulge.

"Stay back now," said Bulge, flashing the thick knife. The boy had passed out on the cobblestones.

The white American tourist wasn't taking orders and continued advancing. Bulge widened his stance, held the backpack under his left arm, and pointed the knife in his right hand at the man.

The tourist wasn't dumb. He bent down, picked up a loose cobblestone the size of a fist, and threw it hard at the assailant.

It landed square in Bulge's sternum. He stumbled

backwards, knocked off balance. The red backpack flew out of his grasp, and he fell to the ground.

The white tourist ran to the backpack and picked it up. Bulge recovered himself enough to pull his arm back and plunge the knife deep into the man's lower back, just above the left kidney.

The tourist fell facefirst onto the cobblestones, the handle of the knife sticking up out of his back. A whisper of a sound escaped from his lips.

Up ahead, a small crowd had begun to form at the top of Coach Lane.

The man they called Bulge scooped up the boy's red backpack for the second time. He carried it in his arms as he ran the opposite way down the lane, towards the docks.

WASHINGTON, D.C.

Cosmo Bennett paced the living room of his home, waiting for the buzzer to sound.

It was a sixth-floor condo in Arlington, Virginia. From his balcony, he enjoyed an excellent view, but Cosmo was too distracted to enjoy much of anything these days. The number-one reason for that was the divorce paperwork resting in his filing cabinet. The number-two reason was the unfinished PowerPoint presentation currently open on his laptop.

He stood at the sliding glass door, hands on hips, looking out across the city. Cosmo Bennett was mid-forties, trim and strong, a little bit edgy. He was dressed in a green field jacket, black jeans, and brown suede Chelsea boots. He wore a close-cropped beard on his face. Above the beard were a pair of aviator sunglasses that reflected the Potomac River, the Lincoln Memorial, and the Washington Monument, stuck into the city like a pin into a map.

The buzzer sounded. Cosmo headed quickly to the intercom, hit the button, and said, "Send him up."

A minute later, a knock at the door. He opened it. Standing there was a chubby kid, early twenties. He wore a Bulbasaur Pokemon t-shirt and a pair of heavy overear headphones. A Jansport backpack hung off one shoulder.

When he saw Cosmo, he pulled himself up straight and yanked the headphones down around his neck.

"Finally," said Cosmo. "I thought I was going to be late for my flight."

"Hey Professor Bennett—"

"Just call me Cosmo," he said. "If you're housesitting for me, we should be on a first-name basis."

Cosmo had a deeper reason for being called by his first name. In his heart of hearts, he didn't feel like a real professor. He'd lived most of his life outside the ivory tower. In fact, he hadn't been planning to join a university at all, but life had taken an unexpected direction.

"I'm sorry, sir—"

Cosmo stepped aside. "Don't call me 'sir' either. Come in."

Noah entered the apartment and took it in. He moved along the row of photos on the credenza. A young Cosmo in a wrestling stance. Skating in a hockey game. Hugging his mother in a basketball uniform.

"You were an athlete?"

"I still am."

"What sport do you like the most?"

"Anything to keep me sane. Exercise is my drug."

The young man nodded. His eyes scanned the room. "This place is pretty dope."

"Thanks. I didn't decorate any of it."

"So your wife did it?"

Cosmo made a circling motion with his hands, his mouth trying to form words. Noah quickly realized his mistake.

"Oh right, they told me about that," he said. Then added: "I don't know what to say. You guys split up, right?"

"Yeah."

He searched for the right words. "I'm sorry for your loss?"

"It's more of a bittersweet win," Cosmo replied. "Follow me."

The older man led the younger one into the kitchen. It boasted a modern urban style—clean surfaces, stainless steel sink, geometric pattern backsplash, and other contemporary finishings. "So, first things first. The keys to everything are on the kitchen table. The code to the garage is fourteen seventeen."

"I don't have a car," said Noah.

"Even better. But don't take mine. Help yourself to whatever half-eaten condiments are in the refrigerator, they're probably expired." Cosmo pointed at the hallway on the other side of the apartment. "You'll sleep in the guest bedroom over there. I don't have pets anymore because she took both of them, so that's easy. And no parties." Cosmo's eyes tracked up and down the young visitor. "But I'm guessing that probably won't be a problem."

"It's gonna be lit, yo," said Noah, shooting a finger gun at the ceiling.

Cosmo shrugged and went into his bedroom. He emerged dragging his suitcase towards the door. "How old are you again, Noah?"

"I'm twenty-two, sir."

"Don't call me sir. First-year graduate student?"

"Yep."

"And we met just that one time at the orientation social hour, right?"

"Yes—"

"Who's your advisor?"

"You are."

Cosmo stopped and looked at him. "Oh."

"I've been trying to get an appointment with you for, like, a month," Noah said. "I saw on the message board that you needed a house sitter. I thought this would be the best way to finally talk to you."

Cosmo ran an embarrassed hand through his hair. "That would be my fault then. I'm sorry."

"I mean, it's all right. Everybody told me you didn't really act like a professor. But they also said you were, like, the best one."

The professor cast his eyes down to the ground. It was good to hear that people were giving him a stamp of approval, even if it was behind his back. It'd been a long time since he felt that anybody had really believed in him.

"What do you think your concentration in geography will ultimately be?" he said.

Noah blew air out of his mouth. "I was hoping you could help me with that."

"Give me your best guess, right now."

"Maybe digitization. Like, the integration of new geospatial tools with pre-existing data frameworks."

"Yeah," said Cosmo.

"Does that sound okay?"

"We'll figure that out later. I want you to look at this." Cosmo held up a finger as he retrieved his laptop, then opened it to his PowerPoint. "I have to deliver this presentation on Saturday. And I don't know what to say about the industry's lack of common data standards given the proliferation of so many new tools. I haven't even used half of them yet."

"Well, you are old," said Noah.

"Thanks. What more can I say other than it's a problem?"

"Maybe offer solutions?"

"Doing that makes me a target. I like to keep a low profile. Do you think you can help?"

Noah shrugged. "I'll do my best."

Cosmo slapped him on the back and closed the laptop. "I'll send it to you from the airport. You can work on that in the next couple of days. I have to deliver it on Saturday."

"Where are you going again?"

Cosmo zipped the computer into his backpack. "The annual meeting of the International Association of Cartographers. It's at a resort on the island nation of Tatuaga, in the eastern Caribbean. It's a six-hour flight, connecting through Miami."

"Lucky you."

Cosmo stuck out his right hand. "Let's talk tomorrow. You've got my number."

Noah reached out and shook it. Cosmo looked down at his hand, puzzled. "Are you feeling okay?"

"Yeah, why?"

"You just … you have a soft handshake."

"I do?"

"Yeah. You wanna try again?"

Rolling his eyes, Noah reached back and thrust his hand into Cosmo's hand, then pumped it twice, hard.

"Much better," Cosmo said. "We'll talk later."

"Yeah, call me whenever."

Noah forced a smile. Cosmo waved goodbye, pulled his suitcase into the hallway, and shut the door.

As his footsteps disappeared down the hallway, Noah collapsed on the sofa, rubbed his eyes with his knuckles, and exhaled.

"I don't know if I'm ready for this," he said.

CHAPTER
THREE

THE ISLAND OF TATUAGA, EASTERN ANTILLES, CARIBBEAN

Cosmo Bennett stepped into the late afternoon tropical sunlight and squinted before descending the staircase to the asphalt tarmac.

This was Tatuaga International Airport. It'd been built in the nineteen-sixties to serve as a regional airport. Since then, however, the island's growing reputation as a tourist destination meant expansion and traffic.

Feeling the heat, Cosmo stripped off his field jacket and wrapped it around his waist. He put on his aviators and made his way over to customs. A large sign on the wall in cursive script read *Welcome to Tatuaga*.

Once inside, he passed through immigration quickly and headed to the baggage claim. A group of three middle-aged white men were standing around the carousel, hands in pockets, chatting happily. Cosmo recognized one of them. He immediately turned sideways, placing his hand up to the side of his face.

Too late. The man waved at him. "Cosmo!"

Cosmo pivoted, pretending to be surprised. Then he

strolled over and shook the man's hand. "Professor Canavan."

"Please—it's Robert."

"How have you been?"

Robert Canavan was the head of a prestigious geography department at a university on the East Coast. It looked as though he'd spent the last thirty years slumped behind a desk. His body was shaped like a question mark. He wore a black blazer, a light blue Oxford button down shirt, shapeless beige slacks, and scuffed brown tassel loafers. He and Cosmo had met at this same conference the previous year, and they'd taken an instant shine to one another.

"Not bad," he said. "I hope your second year in the classroom went better than the first?"

"You could say that."

"And the students?"

"There was improvement," replied Cosmo. "They went from antagonistic to merely bored."

That got a chuckle from the group. "Take whatever you can get," said Canavan. "Do you know Sam Jones and Giancarlo LaRusso? This is Cosmo Bennett."

He shook the other men's hands. Both were about his own age. He got the feeling that this group of professors had been longtime colleagues. Cosmo felt like an interloper.

He was also sure that Robert was going to ask him to explain himself. It made him nervous.

"What's your role here?" said LaRusso. "Attendee or presenter?"

"Almost half of us are presenting," said Jones.

"I'm speaking on Saturday morning," Cosmo said.

"On what?" said LaRusso.

"The usual, GIS tools and frameworks, blah blah blah."

The three professors nodded. Jones said, "Most of us are really here for the beach."

"I can't wait," said Canavan.

"Whoever chose Krakow last year should've been fired," said LaRusso.

"It was Tomas Zielinski, and he died a few months ago," replied Canavan.

"Well, shit," said LaRusso, "I didn't want to go that far."

"Be careful what you wish for," said Jones.

Their baggage was spit out onto the carousel, and the men hauled it onto the floor. A porter was at their side instantly, baggage cart in hand. Cosmo found himself tagging along at the back of the group as they exited the airport. A passenger van with the word Slippers Resorts written on the side waited at the curb.

"Inside, my friends," said Canavan.

"I'll wait for the next one," said Cosmo.

Robert looked at him oddly. "No worries, man. There's plenty of room."

"It's okay."

"I insist, Cosmo. You're one of us."

He sighed. "Are you sure? You guys are such old friends, I'm sure you have plenty to talk about—"

Canavan slapped him on the back. "Shut up and get in."

Cosmo reluctantly climbed inside the van, seating himself next to Canavan. Behind them, the porter hoisted their bags into the rear baggage compartment and closed it. Then the passenger door slid shut and the vehicle began moving through the streets of the island.

"So, Professor Bennett, tell us about yourself," said LaRusso. He and Jones were sitting in the row behind.

There it was. Cosmo clenched his hand. He'd wanted to avoid this.

"Cosmo's career hasn't followed a normal trajectory," said Canavan. "He's kind of the guy we desk monkeys wish we could be."

"How so?" asked LaRusso.

Canavan slid his eyes over. *Do you want to tell them?*

There was no escaping it any longer. Cosmo cleared his throat. "Okay, here's my story. I used to work at the Department of the Interior. I was a cartographer."

"And what happened?" said Jones.

"I was working on a survey map being used by real estate developers. I noticed that my colleagues were failing to mark the use of a filled-in canal for chemical dumping. Very dangerous, right?"

"For sure," said LaRusso.

"I brought this up to the Secretary in one of those ask-me-anything staff roundtables. He ignored me. So I brought it up again a while later with my boss, who told me to back off. So I did. Two weeks later, they fired me." He paused. "I was a GS-13."

That was top level, a career competitive.

"Whoa," said Jones.

"I think I heard about that," said LaRusso. "Somebody said that you fought the good fight."

"It's the only one I ever lost," Cosmo replied.

Canavan said, "So that's how he ended up in academia."

"No," Cosmo said, "in between I took a detour to a private firm that made tourist maps for local chambers of commerce."

"How was that?" asked Jones.

"Misery. I started drinking, my wife was unhappy. Then she finally left. I never got her to come back. After that, the university approached me, mostly out of pity. They hired me, thankfully full-time but non-tenure track. And now here I am."

The van fell silent.

"Well, thank you for your honesty," said LaRusso.

"You've had a rough time," added Jones.

Cosmo drummed his hands on his thighs. "Sorry, I don't mean to bring everybody down."

"On the positive side," said Canavan, "he works out three hours a day and looks to be aging in reverse."

Soon the conversation turned to other topics. Cosmo was pretty sure what the others were thinking. His life story was an object lesson in professional survival. *This is what happens when a man tries to do the right thing.* That man loses his job and his wife and his self-respect.

Problem was, Cosmo hadn't ever been able to just go along. He had too much backbone for that. He liked speaking truth to power. The problem was that power usually knew the truth, because it created truth.

The vehicle snaked down the coastal road for a couple of miles and turned left into the Slippers Resort.

"And we have arrived, my friends," said Canavan.

They stepped out beneath a massive portico. A riot of colorful flowers filled a large ceramic pot in the center of the rotunda.

A valet greeted them. "Here for the cartography conference, gentlemen?"

"Absolutely," said Canavan.

"We will take care of everything for you. Come this way."

Cosmo and the others casually sauntered into the lobby of the resort. It was filled with natural light and bright décor. Beneath their shoes lay a green-and-brown floral carpet, and the sofas were covered in rainbow-striped upholstery. A series of white arches on all four sides beckoned the visitors to explore in every direction.

A young female employee with a white flower in her black hair approached them. She wore a pink blazer and was bearing a silver tray of champagne flutes filled with yellow passionfruit juice.

"Compliments of the resort," she said, smiling.

The men each took one, then turned and toasted one another.

"To Tatuaga!" said Jones.

Cosmo clinked glasses and drank. That's when he noticed the housekeeper beneath one of the arches. Thirtyish, she was small and dark-skinned. Her eyes were two different colors and carried a haunted look. She was folding white towels and stacking them onto a cart that was already stacked high with folded white towels.

And she was studying him.

They made eye contact. The housekeeper took a single towel from her cart and walked over to Cosmo. She laid the towel gently across his forearm and pressed it down.

"Welcome to Slippers, sir," she said in a heavily accented voice. "This is in case you would like to go swimming, sir."

"Thank you," Cosmo said. He noted her name badge read Harriet.

The housekeeper dipped her head slightly and backed away. Then she pushed the cart through one of the arches and disappeared.

"Well goddamn," said LaRusso, "maybe getting divorced has its benefits."

"Go get her, tiger," joked Jones.

The comments slid off Cosmo's back. He'd been approached by many women in his life. He knew how they carried themselves when they were interested. But this one had a different vibe.

He couldn't tell what she wanted, but it intrigued him.

Next morning, Cosmo was on his third set of hanging upside down crunches when he saw the housekeeper enter the fitness center.

Seventy minutes of hard exercise, and Cosmo still wasn't tired yet. He'd done the curls, the squats, the dead-lifts. He'd swung kettlebells. He'd planked for two minutes. He'd rowed the erg so hard that he'd dry heaved into a water fountain afterwards. Some gym rats used notebooks to record their efforts, but Cosmo didn't care about the numbers. All he wanted was to exert himself, over and over, until he couldn't move.

That was how he could forget.

Cosmo knew he was punishing himself. He knew he hadn't forgiven himself for his mistakes. But he also knew that he liked the way it made him feel.

He finished his final set of hanging crunches. Cosmo placed the palms of his hands on the floor, then released the bar from behind his knees. Now he was in a handstand. Stiffening his arms and shoulders, he folded his legs forward until his feet hit the ground. Then he stood up in a swift move. Upright, he closed his eyes and leaned against the wall as the blood rushed out of his head and the dizziness flooded into it.

He stayed like that for a good minute. When he opened his eyes, Harriet was standing before him. She was holding another fresh white towel.

"Hello," she said.

"Hey," he replied, still dizzy.

"You look like you need another towel," she said.

Harriet handed him a towel. Cosmo accepted it and wiped the sweat from his face and neck. "That's very nice of you, Miss Harriet. Are you offering to be my personal servant this week?"

He delivered it with a smile. It was the type of flirty comment that usually won phone numbers and occasionally a heart.

"No," the housekeeper said bluntly. But she kept staring at him. She made no attempt to leave.

Now Cosmo was intrigued. Harriet was running a different game here, no doubt.

"Is there something I can do for you?" he asked.

Harriet chewed on her lower lip, thinking. Then her haunted eyes flicked up to his face with utmost seriousness. "You a geographer?"

"Yeah."

"How long you been doin' that?"

"Twenty-five years."

"What kind of maps you study?"

"All of them. Topographical surveys, isoline, choropleth, dot density, whatever."

The housekeeper had taken control of the conversation now. All Cosmo could do was see where she was leading it.

"My family has something important," she said slowly, "and I want you to explain it to me."

"What is it?"

"I can't tell you."

For a moment, Cosmo thought that this might be the world's most unusual type of come-on. But another look at the pain in her mismatched eyes scrubbed that thought out of his head. This housekeeper carried a weight on her shoulders.

"Okay," he said.

"We have to talk in private," she said.

"That's fine. You want to come by my room?"

Her eyes searched the horizon for moment, thinking. Then she nodded. "I'm off at five pm."

"Perfect," he said.

"Thank you," she replied.

Then Harriet held her hand out, palm up. Cosmo reached out and clasped it.

"I want the towel, Dr. Bennett."

"Oh."

He gave her the towel back. She carried it to her cart and pushed it out of the fitness center. He watched the door close behind her.

Only then did Cosmo realize that she had called him by his name.

The cartographers' conference was held on the mezzanine level of the resort. It was split between six small satellite conference rooms and one main ballroom, where the larger presentations were scheduled to occur.

Cosmo was sitting in the main ballroom right now, surrounded by other professional cartographers, listening to one of those presentations. He wore jeans, moccasins, and a white linen collar shirt with two buttons left open at the top. In his hands was a conference folder; under his seat was a conference swag bag.

The speaker, a professor from Germany who spoke English with ramrod precision, had been droning on for twenty minutes about changes in technology use that could lead to the possibility of a true secant form of the Lambert Conformal Conic projection.

Cosmo wasn't listening. He'd been messaging Noah instead.

> -How's the presentation going N?

> -You were right, it's actually really hard to come up with something that's not a solution

> -I need you to finish it by tomorrow

Noah had replied with a vegetable emoji whose meaning wasn't exactly clear. Cosmo stowed away his phone.

The speaker finally concluded, and the audience applauded. Robert Canavan came up to the podium and leaned into the microphone.

"Before we break," he said, "I just want to remind everybody here about a few of the several exciting speakers coming up over the next few days. Tomorrow, Dr. Stephen Grontar is going to talk about his experience georeferencing a two hundred-and-thirty-year-old map of his hometown near Sheffield in northern England. On Thursday, Dr. Christine Grayland will let us know about some of the challenges she encountered while working with First Nations people in northern Saskatchewan. On Friday, Dr. Prithi Sundaloo will address the decline of the consumer mapping industry."

Cosmo was already stuffing the folder into his swag bag when he heard his name.

"And on Saturday, Dr. Cosmo Bennett will talk about the geospatial industry's lack of common data standards. Stand up and say hello, Cosmo."

Canavan was looking at him, making a stand-up gesture with his hands. Cosmo felt two hundred and fifty faces turn towards him.

Crap.

Cosmo slowly stood up, raised one hand, and swiveled around while mustering the best smile he could for the group.

"He's newly single, ladies," said Canavan, a grin on his face. "You can catch him at the Terrace Bar at happy hour today."

Cosmo shook his head no, drew his finger across his neck.

"No?" said Canavan. "I'm just trying to help, buddy. You obviously need it."

That got some laughter. Cosmo sat down and buried his face in his hands. Being the center of attention was never his favorite state of being. Especially not when his divorce was being brought to the attention of a room of strangers.

Canavan left the stage. The audience rose and began chatting in small groups, but Cosmo quickly headed for the exit.

CHAPTER
FIVE

In his room, Cosmo flopped on his back on the king-sized bed. He began to count the swirls in the ceiling and stopped at sixty. Then he sat up, kicked off his moccasins, and went over to the coffee maker. He filled the water reservoir and slid the packet of grounds into the filter and pressed the on button.

He peeled off his shirt and went into the bathroom and looked at himself in the mirror. Mid-forties, and despite the diet and exercise, his eyes were looking more tired than usual. Part of that was the dehydrating nature of airplane travel, but another part of that could be blamed on the last few years of his life.

Who was he? All his certainty had disappeared. He used to be happy, but that had mostly evaporated. He didn't know anybody his age who was happy either. It seemed like his generation's emotional state had been nose-diving. It wasn't from the pandemic either. Maybe it was the cost of growing older, maybe it was something deeper about Western culture. Regardless, Cosmo knew he needed to turn his life around, if he wanted any chance of finding contentment again.

He splashed water on his face and toweled it off. From the other room he could hear the coffeemaker sucking up the water and dribbling it out into the pot. It was a reassuring sound.

There was a knock at the door.

Cosmo paused for a moment, forgetting who that could be. Then he remembered.

Harriet.

It was five o'clock. He sighed. He wasn't feeling in the mood for a visitor, but he'd agreed to this.

"One minute," he shouted. He went to his suitcase and found a new t-shirt and put it on. He ran a comb through his hair.

Then he opened the door. The housekeeper stood in the hallway, a look of utter seriousness etched onto her face. She'd swapped out her resort-issued polo shirt for a simple gray t-shirt, but she still wore the long black housekeeper pants and black trainers. In her left hand was a shopping bag.

"Come in," he said.

She entered wordlessly. He closed the door behind her.

"Do you want some coffee?"

"No," she said.

"Okay."

Harriet remained on her feet. She seemed as though she were in a different headspace completely. Cosmo wondered if she was all there, mentally.

He poured himself a cup of coffee and sat down at the small table alongside the window. He gestured for her to take the other seat.

Harriet looked around the room. "Can you close the curtains, please?" she said.

Cosmo looked outside. From his balcony was a

gorgeous view of the Caribbean sunset over the ocean. People paid hundreds of dollars a night for that view.

"As you wish," he said.

He rose and pulled the curtains shut. The room grew immediately darker, so he turned on the floor lamp. Now it felt more intimate.

Satisfied, Harriet sat down opposite him at the table. She arranged her legs so her shins were slanted diagonally, crossed at the ankles. She folded her hands on her lap.

"What did you want to show me?" Cosmo said.

"My son was attacked a few days ago," she said, "by a man who stole his backpack."

"I didn't hear about that," he said.

"The tourists are protected from bad news."

"Is he okay?"

"He is still in the hospital, but the doctors said he will survive. The man sliced him across the chest with a knife."

Cosmo winced. "I'm sorry about that."

"The man also killed a tourist who tried to interfere."

"Terrible," said Cosmo. "What prompted this?"

She drew a deep breath. "My family is originally from Guyana. My father was named George, and he came here to Tatuaga over fifty years ago. He died a few months ago, but on his deathbed, he gave my son a small notebook. He said that notebook was worth a fortune. Those were his words exactly. He was very serious about that."

"Your father never mentioned this notebook to you before that?"

Harriet shook her head no. "We had no idea it existed. He kept it a secret all those years."

"What's in the notebook?"

"It's a group of maps. All drawn by hand."

"Did Grandpa George make them himself?"

She nodded.

Cosmo found himself growing more intrigued. "What are the maps of?"

Harriet shrugged. "We don't know. We have some ideas, but he never explained them. He died just two days later. Their secret was taken to his grave. But we know that a man just tried to kill my son to get them."

Cosmo thought about it. "Did this assailant specifically tell your son that he wanted the maps?"

"No. But he said he wanted something in my son's backpack. There was nothing else Desmond could be carrying that would prompt this man to do such a horrible thing. Plus we have investigated and found evidence that he was watching my family for several days. He knew that Desmond was bringing the notebook to school and else-where. Desmond was studying his grandfather's maps everywhere he went the last few weeks."

"But the man didn't get them?"

Harriet dropped her head, a smile appearing on her face for the first time. "Thank the Lord, Desmond forgot the notebook that day. All this terrible man got were some loose papers and some schoolwork."

"Algebra homework isn't really valuable."

"That's right," the woman said, then smiled. It was an authentic expression of happiness. She was as truthful as a person can be.

"So you need my help to decipher these maps," he said.

"Yes, please."

"Why did you choose me? This resort is full of two hundred and fifty cartographers right now."

Her eyes glanced at his body. "The other men look like professors. But you don't look like them. You look like you have faced some danger."

He felt relieved. In three sentences, this housekeeper

had cut through to the very heart of his crisis. Cosmo was in academia, but he wasn't *of* academia. It was good to know that someone could see him for what he was.

He nodded. "So where is Grandpa George's notebook of hand-drawn maps?"

"Here."

Harriet reached into her shopping bag and removed a worn leatherbound notebook. It was held together by a rusted filament of wire.

She carefully handed the object over to him. Cosmo accepted it with reverence. He opened the first page and examined it, chewing on his lip. Harriet watched him expectantly.

Then he looked up. "Can I keep this for a little while? I'm going to need time."

The housekeeper looked hesitant. "Yes, but you must return it."

"Obviously."

"It's very precious."

"I understand. It will stay here on the premises. Maybe you would like to come back tomorrow? At the same time?"

Harriet dipped her head in respect. "I will do that. I thank you in advance, Dr. Bennett. Anything you can tell me will be helpful."

They both rose to their feet. They shook hands quickly, and Harriet went to the door and let herself out.

The door closed. Cosmo found a set of three pencils in his luggage. He turned on his desk lamp and sat down at his chair.

Then he began to study the maps.

CHAPTER
SIX

Downstairs at the Terrace Bar, a hundred and fifty drunk cartographers were making enough noise to fill a football stadium.

The sounds of talking, laughter, singing, roaring—it all amped up, congealed into a cloud of sound, and floated out over the ocean on the other side of the railing.

In the center of the vortex, however, Cosmo Bennett wasn't paying attention to any of it.

He had posted himself at the end of the bar, perched halfway on a stool. One shoe on the footrest, the other on the ground. Before him squatted a collins glass of club soda with a green wedge of lime, soaking in a circle of its own condensation on a napkin.

He held the end of a pencil against his temple with his right hand. On the bar, kept carefully clear of all liquids, was the old man's notebook of hand-drawn maps.

"You good, man?" said a voice.

Cosmo looked up. It was the bartender, a jovial guy in a resort-issued black polo shirt.

"Yeah," he said.

"You don't want a rum sour?"

"No."

"I thought you said you wanted a rum sour."

"I didn't say that," Cosmo replied.

"All right then."

The bartender moved along. Cosmo returned his attention to the maps of Grandpa George from Guyana, whoever he'd been. He'd been studying the man's cartographic work for half an hour.

Cosmo had never seen anything like it.

The collection featured exactly one hundred hand-drawn maps, all bound together in a spiral notebook. The first odd thing about the notebook was the coiled wire. It was irregularly bent, damaged here and there, and soldered to itself at either end. He guessed that Grandpa George had repurposed some wiring from a wall and done it himself.

The second odd thing about the notebook was its size. Each page measured six inches across by nine and a quarter inches long. It wasn't typical size, not by modern standards, but Cosmo could admit he had never studied standard dimensions of stationery in developing countries. He wondered if it'd been cut by hand.

Each page featured the same general pattern. On the top of each page was a date, written day/month/year. Flipping through the notebook, he'd seen that each map was dated approximately a week apart.

The cluster of light bulbs above the bar reflected in Cosmo's eyes as he studied the first map. A land mass had been drawn at the bottom left portion of page, with a black square denoting the starting point for whatever was being tracked. A hand-drawn date, in precise script: *6 March 1973*. From there, a red line had been drawn northeast, to what appeared to be an island, where another date had been written: *8 March 1973*. The red line then jogged to the left, to the northwest, to what appeared to be a larger piece of land. Another date there: *9 March 1973*. Then a final line, again to the northeast, to a smattering of tiny islands. The red line finally stopped on one. A final date: *11 March 1973*.

None of the land masses were marked. None of the distances were measured. In fact, there was no other information, except for three decimals penned very deliberately in the upper right corner. On the first map were 0.6, 1.2, and 1.5. On subsequent maps, the numbers ranged from 0.4 to 2.3.

The final map was marked *January 27, 1975*.

George had drawn these maps for almost two years. What had he been tracking?

Cosmo tapped his pencil against his teeth. The red lines didn't vary by width, and it wasn't clear that they were flow maps. It's possible that the items being measured stayed consistent, but not likely.

He was stumped.

A hand landed on Cosmo's shoulder. He looked up into the reddened face of Robert Canavan. Behind him, Jones and LaRusso grinned, both holding tall rum drinks.

"I thought you weren't coming down for happy hour," said Canavan.

"I wasn't," said Cosmo, "until I was given this notebook of old maps. I figured the two hundred cartographers here might be able to help me."

He turned the notebook towards his colleague.

"Well," said Canavan, "I'm always happy to help a colleague in need." He withdrew his reading glasses from his pocket and placed them onto his face. "Let's see what we have."

Robert leaned in, his belly lopping onto the counter. His lips parted slightly as he studied the map.

"How many?" he said.

"There's a hundred."

"Exactly?"

"I think so."

"All dated?"

"Meticulously. Each one week apart. They're from the nineteen seventies."

Cosmo flipped through the notebook. On each map, his finger traced the same red route zigzagging between the islands.

"Boats," Canavan said. "That's my guess. These are probably nautical records. They look like shipping routes."

LaRusso said, "But navigational maps were much better than this in the nineteen seventies."

Jones peered down at the notebook over Canavan's shoulder. "This mapmaker was poor. You can tell."

LaRusso agreed. "It's a home job."

"He was from Guyana," said Cosmo. "He passed away a few months ago."

"But a very precise record keeper," said LaRusso. He elbowed Canavan out of the way, then pointed to the large land mass on the lower left. "That resembles Guyana's coastline, kind of. That indentation could be the mouth of the Essequibo. But these islands"—his fingers danced over the smattering of tiny land masses in the upper right—"are a mystery."

"There's no compass rose," said Canavan.

"It could be pointing north," said Jones.

"Or he might've rotated it to fit the paper."

The jovial bartender made eye contact with Cosmo again. That was all the excuse he needed.

"How's the club soda, man? Good?"

"Oh yeah."

"You sure I can't get you anything else?"

"Not right now."

"We have a policy, my friend. Everybody here orders a rum drink at least once, or else they have to meet my friend Chester."

"Who's Chester?"

The bartender turned and pointed to a machete hanging on the wall behind him.

"That's Chester," he said. Then he bellowed and slapped his knee.

Cosmo relaxed. The manager seemed like the type who enjoyed more independence from corporate than others did.

"My friend will take a rum sour," said Canavan. "He's getting over a breakup."

The bartender stared at Cosmo. "Why didn't you say so?" he said bartender, indignation. He spread his arm out towards the bottles of liquor. "We have an entire pharmacy to help cure that affliction—and I am the head pharmacist."

"Thanks," mumbled Cosmo.

A moment later, the rum sour landed on the counter. Another round of cheers followed, with the three professors holding their drinks in the air. Cosmo quietly closed the notebook and stowed it away.

CHAPTER
SEVEN

WASHINGTON, D.C.

Noah sat on the edge of Cosmo's black couch, the large overear headphones gripping his skull, the microphone flipped down to his mouth. In his hands was a video game controller. The blue light of Cosmo's large-screen television was reflected in his face.

"You're not listening to me," he was saying to the other player. "If we go left into the sand bunker without the flamethrower power pack, then that Perpatrod is gonna have us for lunch. It's that centipede-tiger hybrid thing we saw in stage fourteen. Of course I know what I'm talking about! Bro, that's ridiculous, nobody's deployed the powder keg yet in this stage, okay? So that whole class of guardian is at full strength. It's just, like, I've played this game so many times—hey wait, hang on, I have a call."

He touched a button on the side of his headphones. "Yeah?"

"Noah, it's Cosmo."

The graduate assistant scrambled to his feet. "Dr. Bennett, I was just—"

"—playing video games?"

Noah tossed the controller aside and assumed an air of professionalism. "Well, isn't that kind of presumptuous, I mean—"

"Nobody your age answers phone calls that quickly unless they're using game chat on PlayStation."

It's Xbox, Noah mouthed silently. Then: "If this is about the presentation, I am working on it as we speak—"

"Good to know, but it isn't. I need your help with something else."

Noah relaxed. He sauntered into Cosmo's kitchen and opened a bag of chips. "Okay. What's up?"

"I have a set of strange maps, about a hundred of them, that need some analysis."

Noah stuffed a handful of chips into his mouth. "I can take a look at them, sure."

"Stop eating my snacks and listen to me," said Cosmo.

Noah closed the bag and put it away. "I'm listening."

"These are hand-drawn maps that nobody can understand, not even a conference of professional cartographers. I need you to help me find a way to analyze them. One of those … new tools."

"You mean AI tools."

"Yeah, those."

"Okay, sure."

Cosmo paused. "That's all you have to say?"

"I mean, it's not hard. Some tools are open and free because your data is more valuable to them than their service is to you. For the better ones like GeoDingusAI you need a subscription."

"Can we use that one?"

"Yeah."

"How do we buy a subscription?"

"The department already has one. I'm sorry, Dr. Bennett, but shouldn't you know that?"

"Not right now, Noah. Listen, I just sent you the first ten maps. You run them through the tools, and then you tell me what you find. Get to your laptop."

Noah scurried over to his laptop on Cosmo's kitchen table. He sat down, wiped his hands on his pants, then opened up his browser.

"You want me to call you back when this is done?" he said.

"No," said Cosmo, "I'll just wait. I like the feeling of you squirming."

"I will squirm my best then." Noah's fingers danced over the keyboard as he logged onto email, downloaded the attachments, logged onto GeoDingusAI, and uploaded the photos of the maps.

"How should we prompt it?" Noah said.

"No idea. I just want to know what I'm looking at."

Noah thought on that. Then he shrugged and typed What am I looking at?. Then he submitted the query.

"Okay," he replied, "now we just wait a few seconds."

"All right."

Beep. A paragraph arrived in the answer field.

"Got it," said Noah. He leaned forward, squinting. "It returned three interpretations, and each one has a statistical possibility associated with it."

"Read them off to me."

"A map tracking the movement of dolphin pods," Noah said, "eight percent possibility."

"Okay, next," said Cosmo.

"A map of nautical shipping charts, seventeen percent possibility."

"And the last one?"

"A map of bird migration, ninety-three percent possibility."

Silence on the other end of the line. Cosmo said, "There's a ninety-three percent possibility that these are maps of bird migrations?"

"That's what it says."

"But they told me these maps are supposed to be worth a fortune."

"Theoretically, anything's possible—"

"Not with birds! They're disposable. You know what, Noah? I think your software is wrong."

Noah handled him gently. "It's not my software, Dr. Bennett. It's a huge omniscient brain that's been trained on four trillion pieces of geographical data."

"Ask it something else."

"What?"

"The place it was going. The destination."

"Okay." Noah typed: *If the bird migration theory is true, what are the names of the origin and destination?* Then he submitted the question.

Beep. The answer came back instantaneously. *The name of the location of origin is Guyana. The name of the destination is Cragpit Island.*

"It says the origin is Guyana."

"We guessed that."

"It says the destination is Cragpit Island."

Silence at the other end. Noah waited for response.

"Cragpit Island," repeated Cosmo.

"That's correct."

"Well, I guess that's good for now. I'm going to sleep. How's the condo holding up?"

"It's doing great, I guess?" Noah made a what-the-hell face.

"Please get on that presentation. I'll edit it first thing in the morning."

"Right away, sir."

"Don't call me sir."

"Sorry. Good night, taskmaster."

Noah pressed a button on his headphones and hung up. He sighed. Then he went back to the sofa, sat down, picked up the controller, and looked at the screen. His avatar was dying a slow death by digestion inside the intestines of the Perpatrod.

Noah clicked back into the voice chat. "See, what did I tell you would happen? Start the game over, dumbass."

CHAPTER
EIGHT

THE ISLAND OF TATUAGA, EASTERN ANTILLES, CARIBBEAN

Next day at eleven o'clock in the morning, Cosmo stepped out of the Slippers transfer van. He was in the downtown portion of Tatuaga. The island was small enough so that the city didn't need its own name. Everybody just called it the city.

This was billed as a two-and-a-half-hour exploration of the local cuisine. Eight other conference attendees were on the excursion, none of whom he recognized. The tour was designed to get the participants back to the resort in time for the afternoon sessions in the main ballroom.

As Cosmo followed the group down the cobblestone streets, however, two words kept echoing through his mind.

Cragpit Island.

Before falling asleep, he'd checked an online map of the region on his phone, but Cragpit Island was evidently so small that it hadn't appeared anywhere. It was also possible that the AI tool that Noah used was confused. It wouldn't be the first time that AI had given inaccurate or even wrong responses.

Ahead, the tour leader, Jody, was walking backwards, describing the island. The history of Tatuaga was much like many others in the region. Indigenous people slaughtered by the arriving Spanish. Swapped repeatedly by European powers. The importation of African slaves for manual labor. A failed slave rebellion. Declaration of independence from the colonial power. And the final transformation into a tourist service economy.

This is how it went in the Caribbean.

They stopped at a fritter stand, and Jody struggled to explain why the people of Tatuaga had come to enjoy the small fried balls of dough so much. The explanation wasn't really satisfying, and neither was the conch fritter, which Cosmo thought was too oily.

Cragpit Island. The words were stuck in his head like the melody of an insipid pop song.

Jody guided the group to a small takeout counter that specialized in oxtail stew. It wasn't strictly an island specialty, but the people of Tatuaga put their own spin on it with generous amounts of tipcranny, a local orange pepper. The small paper cups of stew made their way around the group.

After the fourth stop, Cosmo lost attention. He found himself wanting to chat with locals.

About Cragpit Island.

He spotted a bar down a side street. It had faded turquoise clapboard siding. The people standing outside it didn't have a care in the world.

This was the type of place he needed to go, and not for the rum.

Cosmo quickly ran alongside the tour leader. "Jody," he said, "I'm kind of full. I'm going to step off the tour for a bit. I'll see you back at the van at one-thirty."

"Be careful," she said.

He nodded. "Always."

Cosmo turned tail and ducked back down the side street. Here the cobblestones were rounder and higher, less smoothed. The bar was basically a rum shack, with locals on the street chatting through the open windows with locals inside.

He headed inside. The smell of sugar, fried fish, and ripe midday body odor hit his nostrils. It wasn't unpleasant. An old refrigerator was branded with a Coca-Cola sign from the 1950s. A pair of fans whirled overhead.

The people watched him. They were used to tourists, but not to a tourist who carried himself so casually into their local places. He seated himself on a shaky wooden stool at the edge of the bar, smack in the middle of the room. A lady with rolled-up sleeves came around. "What ya havin' love?" she said.

"A glass of rum. Do you have fritters?"

"A few."

"I'll take three. And a bottle of water."

She tipped her head up at him to show she understood. Cosmo spun around in his seat. He'd ceased to be an object of interest to the people, who were now chatting amongst themselves. An elderly man near the door sat with his bony hand on a cane like a dark brown piece of gnarled driftwood. A pair of oversized glasses on his face magnified his eyes so that he looked a little alarmed. The man's wife sat beside him, her hand wrapped protectively around his own. She had made herself pretty that morning, and she smiled at Cosmo warmly. Two coffees rested on the table before them.

"What you doin' today my man?"

It came from the fellow next to him. He was thin and wore a red t-shirt with shorts and flip-flops, the classic outfit of the region. But the man hadn't turned his body or his face towards Cosmo. He was the type of guy who preferred not to see his conversation partners.

"Taking a break," replied Cosmo. "I'm here for a conference."

"Where that?"

"Slippers."

The man grunted. "My daughter used to work there. She didn't like it."

"It seems okay. Except the barman. Last night he introduced me to his machete."

That made the man grin. "I know who you are talking about. That's Arthur. He love to play."

The lady with the rolled-up sleeves brought his water, rum, and three fish fritters on a plate. Cosmo made a show of eating one of the deep-fried dough balls. He drank the water and sipped at the rum. The man next to him remained facing straight ahead.

"Can I ask a question?" he said.

"If you'd like," the man replied. His tone was neither friendly nor interested, but Cosmo decided to proceed.

"Have you heard of Cragpit Island?"

The man thought about it. Then his mouth turned into an upside-down semi-circle, and he shook his head. "I don't know it."

The lady with the rolled-up sleeves overheard them. "What's that you asking about?"

"Cragpit Island."

She repeated the name. "Cragpit Island. I don't know it. Is it nearby?"

"I have no idea. Maybe."

A deep, rough, old man's voice cut through the din. "Dat Bird Island."

Cosmo turned around. It was the ancient creature

sitting near the door, with the gnarled hand and the too-large glasses.

"Bird Island?" Cosmo said.

The old man nodded. His wife looked concerned but said nothing.

Bird Island. Cosmo's mind raced.

A map of bird migration.

The lady with the rolled-up sleeves looked stricken. "Why you come in here askin' after Bird Island?"

"I wasn't."

"That's what you just asked about, yeah?"

"I didn't know it went by a different name."

The woman with the rolled-up sleeves made a quick spitting sound between her two front teeth. It was the type of sound an animal makes when it attacks. Then she circled around and yanked away Cosmo's plate of fritters and glass of rum.

The man sitting next to Cosmo turned away from him, slipped off his stool, and moved to an empty table far across the bar.

Evidently it was a sore spot. Cosmo had asked the wrong question and triggered some local ire.

"I'm sorry," he said, under his breath. He pulled out his wallet and left some EC cash on the counter, then walked towards the exit.

A hand grabbed his wrist just before he stepped out. He looked down. It was the old man's wife.

"Don't go to Bird Island," she said.

Cosmo felt his heart rate accelerate. This couple knew something. He crouched down beside them so that his face was lower than theirs.

"I wasn't planning to," he said. "What do you know about it?"

"There's only but one family that lives there," she said, "and they are wealthy but hostile."

"What is their name?"

She looked to her husband, who shook his head no. She leaned over and whispered to Cosmo. "Rumor has it, one of them came here and killed somebody many years ago." She paused for dramatic effect. "There is a history."

Cosmo was intrigued now. "What else can you tell me?"

The woman sensed that she'd spoken too much. She said nothing more, her lips sealed tightly against her face.

"Thank you," Cosmo said.

He stood up and left the rum bar. All the way back to the resort, he thought about Bird Island.

CHAPTER
NINE

At five o'clock pm, Cosmo was pacing his room. A pot of coffee was burbling away on the desk. He was chewing tiny shreds of his fingernails. It was a terrible habit, one that he'd tried to shake for years.

He was waiting for that knock on the door, but it didn't come. He poured himself a cup of coffee and stirred some sugar into it.

Cragpit Island was also called Bird Island.

A ninety-three percent possibility the maps showed bird migration.

His mind was spinning faster and faster. This is how he'd felt as a boy when he'd managed to put together the four edges of a large jigsaw puzzle. Enough to see that the frame of the picture, but not enough to feel he was anywhere near the end.

Fifteen minutes passed, and still no sign of Harriet. He pulled out his phone.

How's the presentation going, N

Almost done

I need it tonight

On it

Cosm0 frowned. That came a little too quick, and a little too easy.

Then the room phone rang. He leapt across the bed and jammed it into the pocket between his ear and his shoulder. "Hello?"

"Dr. Bennett?"

"Yes."

"It's Harriet. Something urgent has come up and I cannot meet you as we had planned."

"Oh. I have some news for you."

"Is that so?"

"Yes."

"I would like to hear it in person. You can meet me tonight at eight-thirty at Reef Beach."

Cosmo didn't like the sound of that. It felt suspiciously like a setup.

"Tell me what's going on," he said.

"I can't tell you just yet. It would be bad luck."

He sighed. "Eight-thirty tonight. Reef Beach."

"Yes, it's the soonest I can meet. Please bring the notebook as well. Thank you."

Cosmo hung up the phone and stared at the steaming coffee cup for a moment. If he was going to consider going to an unfamiliar locals' beach at night, carrying a potentially valuable object, it could only mean one thing.

The mystery of Grandpa George's maps had really gotten its hooks into him.

Down at the Terrace Bar, the conference crowd was in full roar. Cosmo threaded his way through the people, nodding at some, saying hello to others. He turned his body sideways to slip through conversation circles.

Finally, he reached the bar. The barman was setting up a row of four rainbow-colored tiki drinks.

"Hi Arthur," he said.

"How," the barman replied, "have you learned my name."

"I'm full of surprises."

"Your recuperation is going well?"

Cosmo sat on the stool. "Much better, thanks to you. I'd like to order a couple of things."

"Two drinks? Now you talkin' my language."

"First, I want another rum sour."

"That can be arranged. And the second?"

Cosmo pointed to the machete behind the bar. "I'd like to borrow Chester for a while."

The barman raised an eyebrow. "Chester is very particular about friendships. What do you want him for?"

"Protection. I have to go somewhere tonight. Off property."

The insinuation of danger was clear. The bartender studied Cosmo. "Why don't you just stay here? Enjoy yourself." He twirled a finger around the bar. "Socialize with your colleagues."

"I'm trying to help somebody."

"You don't need to be helping anybody on Tatuaga. We take care of ourselves."

Arthur delivered the rum sour, and Cosmo took a sip. "It's missing something."

"What's that?"

"A machete." Cosmo laid a fifty-dollar bill on the

counter. "A boy was slashed across the chest. I'm trying to bring justice. Your help would be greatly appreciated."

Arthur looked at the cash. "I heard about that."

Then he turned and pulled the machete down from behind the bar. He laid it on the countertop. It was longer than Cosmo's forearm.

"You keep your money," he said. "Just be sure you protect each other."

Cosmo made a praying gesture and bowed briefly. "Thank you, Arthur. I do have just one more problem."

"Okay."

Cosmo swiveled around and looked at the crowd. "How am I going to get out of this crowded bar with it?"

The barman laughed. "You won't have any problem with that." He gestured towards the exit, as if to say go ahead.

Cosmo lifted the machete in one hand, grasped his drink in the other, then slipped off his chair. The crowd parted, in fear and in curiosity, as he made his way out.

At the exit, he turned and saluted Arthur with the weapon. The barman saluted back.

CHAPTER
TEN

The taxi arrived at the Reef Beach parking lot just before eight-thirty. Cosmo stepped out and paid the driver. Then he left, and Cosmo found himself alone.

In his backpack was Grandpa George's notebook.

And a machete.

It was almost totally dark here, save for the dim street-lights on the road. The smell of saltwater coiled itself in his nostrils, and the cool trade winds fluttered his shirt.

He picked his way down a path ridged with grass, which soon spat him out onto the ribbon of sand. This was Reef Beach. It stretched about two hundred meters in either direction. At one end lay a jumbled pile of rocks. At the other end a small hotel shone warm and yellow, elevated above the dark sand.

Cosmo listened to the sound of waves crashing hypnot-ically. There wasn't a soul here, other than himself. The locals had stayed home tonight. He allowed his shoulders to drop. He'd been worried over nothing.

Then he saw a figure moving towards him, out of the darkness, down the beach. As it grew closer, Cosmo saw a second figure materialize behind the first. He tensed. Then a third, and a fourth.

This felt like a setup. He cursed himself for having trusted the housekeeper, for having involved himself in this scheme.

Before long, he'd counted fourteen humans moving towards him across the sand. He unzipped his backpack and removed the machete and held it in his hand.

"Stop right there," he shouted.

No response. The figures continued to draw closer. His mind went racing into all sorts of paranoid caves. Harriet had sent people to kill him. He couldn't be allowed to live with the secret of Grandpa George's maps.

"I mean it," he said. Cosmo lifted the machete to show the seriousness of his intention.

"You can put that down," a voice said.

The group were close enough now for him to make out the faces in the faint light from the street. Not threatening, not friendly. These were normal people, if a little sad.

One of the faces he recognized.

Harriet.

The housekeeper stepped to the front to the group, where her eyes found his long knife. "What are you doing with that, Dr. Bennett?"

"I was being safe. Who are these people?"

"This is my family. The Samaroo."

She stepped aside and gestured to three middle-aged men. "These are my brothers. This is William, the oldest. Then John Boy and George Jr."

The three men stepped forward to shake Cosmo's hand. Their grips were strong and their hands were callused. He sensed that the brothers were not people of abstraction. They were men of action.

"No worries about the weapon," said another man. He

was younger, very fit, tall and broad-shouldered. "Bad things happen on this beach at night."

"This is my nephew, Samuel," said Harriet. "He is a swimmer."

"My pleasure," said Cosmo, shaking hands.

"I had to leave work early because my son was discharged from the hospital today," Harriet explained. "We all came down to attend to the cairn for his recovery." She pointed down the beach to a pile of artfully balanced rocks. It was barely visible in the darkness.

"It's a Samaroo tradition when someone is recuperating," another person said. "Our family used to do it in Guyana."

"The afflicted person is supposed to put the final stone on the cairn," another said.

"Tell the boy I'm pulling for him," Cosmo said.

"You can tell him yourself," said William.

The family parted, and someone brought forward the child. It was Desmond. By the dim streetlight, Cosmo could make out his face, his big serious eyes, his gangly limbs. A blue fabric brace had been stretched across his shoulders and chest, immobilizing them, probably so he wouldn't break the stitches that crossed his chest. He seemed like an ordinary kid who'd survived something frightening and consequently lost some of his innocence.

"You look like you're bouncing back nicely," said Cosmo.

"Thank you," Desmond said quietly. Then he turned away and stood behind his mother.

"The doctors think so too," Harriet said. "We've been told he's going to be fine."

"Hey Desmond," said Cosmo, "I have something that belongs to you." He produced the notebook from his bag and handed it to the boy. Desmond snatched it with a bit more force than necessary.

"Take it nice," said Samuel, "the man is a friend."

"So you have some news, Dr. Bennett?" said Harriet.

"I do," replied Cosmo.

The fourteen figures shuffled closer, the sand squeaking beneath their feet. He could see most of the faces more clearly now. They were all focused on what he was about to share.

"It is likely," Cosmo said, "that the maps given to me by Harriet describe a pattern of bird migration."

A moment passed as the group processed this.

"Bird migration," said someone.

"Yes," Cosmo replied. "There is a ninety-three percent possibility, according to the analytic tools we used."

The family members all looked at one another.

"Grandpa George liked pigeons," one said.

"That's true," said another.

"He had quite a few when he was younger," added a third.

"That don't mean nothing, all the miners kept birds—"

"I remember him talking a lot about the hoatzin—"

"What is that?"

"It's the national bird!"

"National bird's a pheasant—"

"—it lives in the mangroves—"

"Boy, I've not been back there since I was Desmond's age—"

"Well, that's too bad for you—"

Cosmo cleared his throat and raised his voice. "I also discovered something else."

The chatter died down as the family members turned their attention back to him.

"On each of the maps," he explained, "the origin of

the bird, if that's what it is, was most likely Guyana. The destination for the bird, if that's what it is, was likely Cragpit Island."

Silence.

"Never heard of it," said John Boy.

"Where is it?" asked George Jr.

"Cragpit Island goes by another name," answered Cosmo. "It's also called Bird Island."

That drew some grumbles. A few of the family members turned away, hands against their foreheads.

"That's a dangerous place," one said.

"We don't like that island at all," said another.

Cosmo raised his voice. "Question. Did Grandpa George love you?"

The group all nodded.

"He loved you all without a doubt?"

"Absolutely," said William. "He was the patriarch. We were his flesh and blood. No one else."

"Then it's obvious," Cosmo replied. "The reason he didn't talk about this because he was trying to protect you from whatever sits on Bird Island."

CHAPTER
ELEVEN

The next morning, in a small conference room at the resort, a professor of cartography at Durham University was pointing to the screen with a red laser pointer. She was explaining something about tapestry segmentation in census data.

Cosmo was seated on a cushioned ballroom chair, with thirty professors to his right, left, front and back. Their faces were held attentively high as they listened. Several were taking notes.

But Cosmo's mind was many miles away.

Thirty-one miles, to be precise.

At Bird Island.

He scrolled through a Google search on his phone. It had yielded almost nothing in the way of clues about the island. There seemed to be no record of it.

Then he remembered there was another resource, far away, sitting in his home and eating his chips. He messaged.

> Noah, I need your help. Bird Island, bird migration, Guyana, fortunes. Connection?

not sure what you mean

find a connection

random but okay

Cosmo lowered his phone and tipped his face upwards and exhaled. It came out louder than expected. The older woman next to him gave him side-eye.

"Shush," she said.

"I'm sorry," he whispered, "I'm having a crisis."

She looked at him. "I remember you. You were at the Terrace Bar the other night. You were studying a notebook."

His phone beeped.

look gotta be honest I don't understand exactly what you want rn

Cosmo sighed. "I have this grad student who is great with tech, but he doesn't understand people."

"Oh, they're all like that now," she whispered. "Show me the puzzle and maybe I can help."

Cosmo tilted the phone towards her. She peered down through her reading glasses at the keywords in the message. "My goodness."

"It's a long shot."

She removed the spectacles. "Well, I do love a good crossword. Any more clues?"

Then Cosmo remembered what someone had said on the beach last night. Grandpa George told me that all the miners kept birds.

"And miners," he added. "I heard someone say miners yesterday."

The woman repeated the words. "Guyana, bird migration, fortunes, and miners?"

Cosmo nodded. He was already texting Noah.

> and miners

"I keep thinking about canary in the coal mine," the woman whispered.

"Those were used by miners to detect poisonous gases," Cosmo whispered back. "That can't be related to fortunes."

At the front of the room, the speaker paused. She looked directly at Cosmo. "Please, whatever you're discussing—could it wait until I'm finished?"

Cosmo held up an apologetic hand. "I'm very sorry."

"Thank you."

He made a zipping motion across his lip and stowed his phone in his pocket. The professor next to him looked mortified.

What he didn't see, flashing onto the screen of the phone in his pocket, was another message from Noah.

> maybe this?

Under it was a link to an article in a history journal. Its title was *Smuggler Pigeons*.

Two hours later, Cosmo held a half-eaten fish sandwich in his hand. He was busy telling a rousing tale about the time he'd nearly been railroaded into working as a drug mule. It was a good story, one he'd entertained people with many times before. It highlighted some of his best qualities—adventurousness, intelligence, physicality, and a dollop of luck.

Around him sat a group of five professors. All strangers, the group were sharing a table on the outside terrace of the resort. The skies were gray, and the pitter-patter of rain sounded against the striped balcony cover that stretched overhead. The gunmetal gray ocean waited, unnaturally calm, against the pilings on the other side of the railing.

Cosmo finished the story. "That sounds like quite an adventure," said one.

"You're presenting tomorrow, aren't you?" said another.

"I am," Cosmo said.

"I hope it's just as entertaining."

"No possibility," he said. "I'll hit the academia switch in my brain. In fact, if anybody wants me tonight, I'll be in my room. Do not disturb please. I need to stay one hundred percent focused."

The conversation wended onwards. Cosmo excused himself to the bathroom. There, standing at the urinal, he remembered his exchange with Noah.

After washing his hands, he fished his phone out of his pocket and looked at the most recent message, then clicked on the link.

Smuggler pigeons.

His eyes scanned the article. His mind ran through the keywords again.

Guyana, bird migration, fortunes, miners.

Bird Island.

Then he remembered the old woman in the café. "There's only but one family that lives there, and they are wealthy but hostile."

As Cosmo began to put it all together, his mouth fell open.

CHAPTER
TWELVE

In the locals' neighborhood at the top of the road, the man they called Bulge crouched beside a patch of love vines, obscured from sight. The ochre-brown skin of his face was slick with sweat. His small tongue wetted itself at the corners of his mouth. His eyes were hidden behind his wraparound sunglasses.

He was studying the house in front of him.

It was a large bungalow, with a pair of wings nestled against the side of the hill on either side of the main house. The front entrance seemed to be well fortified. A security camera was mounted above the front door, for maximum intimidation. The door itself appeared solid and would be tough to break down, even for him. A white Suzuki had been parked off to the left side of the house.

Bulge blew air out of the ring of his mouth. Then he glanced over his shoulder, back down the mountain to the ocean where his dinghy bobbed, just a hundred meters off the beach. They hadn't dared to dock in the port again.

He turned his thick head back to the house. A sound caught his attention. A screen door opened near the end of the righthand wing, and an old woman tottered outside.

The grandmother wore a long drapey yellow t-shirt and jean shorts rolled up to mid-thigh. Her plastic sandals shuffled on the dirt as she slowly crossed the property. Bulge noticed the keys in her hand.

She was walking towards the white Suzuki. This was his opportunity.

Bulge waited for her to pass. Then he rose from behind the vines. His massive body glided silently towards the door on the right wing of the house. His feet minced across the ground, stray pebbles skittering quietly.

He found the screen door unlocked and the heavy interior door wide open. He looked over his shoulder. The old lady was bent over inside her backseat, searching for something.

Bulge entered the house.

The dim corridor was lined with concrete blocks. The only light came from the few open doors at the far end. Bulge turned the doorknob on the first room and looked inside. It was storage. He closed the door.

He was searching for a child's room.

A boy's room.

He methodically checked behind every door in the hallway. One was a girl's bedroom, judging from the frilly pink blanket and princess plush toys. Bulge backed out quickly. Another belonged to an elderly person, maybe the grandmother. It held a rocking chair, a humidifier, and a rainbow-colored weekly pill organizer.

He opened the second-to-last door and paused. This was a boy's room. Model Lego spaceships hung in the air, suspended from the ceiling by fishing line. A large poster of a famous Caribbean singer had been taped to the far wall.

A toy racetrack had been dismantled and the pieces stacked in the corner.

On the desk were several folders and a few books. His huge mitts began pushing them around.

"What is this?" said a voice.

He turned. The grandmother was facing him. In her hand was a knife.

"Not your business," he said.

The woman's face twisted itself into a rage. She shuffled towards him as fast as she could, the knife point held out towards him. He caught her wrist easily and wrenched her arm in a wide arc down to her leg. The knife clattered on the ground.

"You!" she shouted. "It's you!"

Her free hand began to assail him on the chest, but the blows were tiny. The man they call Bulge shoved the old woman backwards. She flew out the door and crashed into the concrete block wall on the opposite side of the hall. Her body slid to the floor. A thin trickle of blood ran down the edge of her jawline and onto her yellow shirt.

Bulge went back to the room. He proceeded to ransack every drawer. He swiped objects off the shelves.

The grandmother had begun to crawl towards the knife on the floor. Bulge noticed. He went into the hallway and stepped on her wrist. Bones cracked audibly. She cried out in pain.

He checked his wristwatch. "I want those maps," he said.

"They not yours," she cried, through gritted teeth.

"I will come back."

"No."

"I will. You know it."

The man called Bulge kicked the knife to the far end of

the hallway. Then he stepped over the prostrate woman, walked down the corridor, and left the house.

Outside, the sunlight shone on his bald head as he descended the side of the mountain, keeping to the same little-used donkey path that he'd used to ascend earlier in the day.

Half an hour later, Bulge was in his dinghy. The motor started up and he pointed it towards the yacht waiting for him out in the water.

CHAPTER
THIRTEEN

Phone to ear, Cosmo ran through the lobby like a man on fire. He'd completely forgotten about his lunch.

"Come on, Noah," he said, "pick up—"

It went to voicemail. Cosmo waited, then left a message: "Noah, I need every map you can find of Cragpit Island. I don't care what types. Elevation, contour, historical, whatever. Call me back."

He stowed his phone away. A member of the housekeeping staff was dusting a planter in the lobby.

"Excuse me," said Cosmo, "can you tell me where Harriet is? I need to speak with her."

The woman fixed him with big eyes. "The Harriet who work here in the laundry?"

"Exactly. I need her. Where do I go?"

She pointed to the left. "The laundry that way."

Cosmo raced across the colorful tropical print carpet and towards a discreet door marked Employees Only. He pushed it open and burst down the functional corridor. The smell of detergent and the sound of whirring machinery told him that he was headed towards the right place.

He turned a corner and found himself in the laundry room. Six washing machines hummed on the right, six dryers spun on the left. Three members of the staff were busy—one folding, one mopping, one texting. They all wore matching black resort outfits.

One lifted her eyes. "You need something?"

"I need Harriet," he said.

"You can't be here," another said.

"Nobody cares about that," said Cosmo. "Where is Harriet?"

"Harriet," the woman shouted back over her shoulder, "there's a man here for you."

The door to a supply closet opened, and out stepped Harriet, looking tired.

"Dr. Bennett," she said, "what's happening?"

He ran around and took her by the shoulders. "I figured it out! I know what the maps are."

Her eyes flicked to her coworkers, who were listening to every word. "Come in here."

Harriet gestured to the supply closet. Cosmo followed her inside. Four simple shelving units lined the four walls. Each was filled with rolls of toilet paper, stacks of coffee packets, small complimentary soaps, and other tiny bits of resort life.

She closed the door. It was dead silent in here, minus the sound of the florescent light buzzing quietly overhead.

"Tell me," she said.

"Last night, someone in your family said that your father had been a miner," Cosmo said.

"Yes, that's right."

"He worked in the mines, in Guyana, correct?"

"Correct."

"In the mines themselves. Like, with a pickaxe?"

The housekeeper nodded. "He said he hated the work and that's why he came here."

"You never told me that," said Cosmo.

She shrugged. "I didn't think of it."

"There are a lot of gemstones in Guyana."

"Oh, there are many. Many many gemstones."

Cosmo balled his hands into excited fists. "Okay, the maps are bird migrations, right? Can we assume that?"

"If you say so."

"Here's my thought. What if your father was using birds to smuggle gemstones out of the mine where he worked?"

Cosmo explained how miners across the world, from Mongolia to South Africa, sometimes brought pigeons into the mines by smuggling them inside their coats or lunch boxes. When they found a gemstone, they would secretly attach the valuable rock to the leg or the neck of the bird, and then release it. The bird would fly out of the mine.

"Fly back home?" said Harriet.

"Or to wherever they trained it to go," said Cosmo.

"Daddy always said you can train some birds," she said. "He said you just had to do it when they're young."

"So maybe he didn't work alone. Maybe he had a friend who imprinted himself on the birds. Maybe this friend trained them to fly to Bird Island."

Harriet's mouth opened. She looked as though she were viewing a sunrise for the first time. "My goodness," she said. "So the way you describe it, this fortune is what exactly?"

"My guess is raw gemstones," Cosmo answered. "And they belong to your family. It's very possible that they're just sitting out there on Bird Island."

"Maybe."

"I could be wrong. There's only one way to find out."

"That's impossible. Nobody goes to Bird Island," Harriet said.

"Then it's time to change that," answered Cosmo, his eyes dancing. "All you need is a boat and a plan."

CHAPTER
FOURTEEN

Cosmo stuck his index fingers inside his ears, keeping out the noise that had erupted here in the living room of Harriet's home.

It was seven o'clock that night. Cosmo and Harriet had shared a tuk-tuk back up the mountain to her family's house. Stepping out, he'd been expecting a ramshackle structure made of blocks. Instead, he was surprised to find a large bungalow with four bedrooms, a spacious modern kitchen, and an enormous living room filled with several pieces of old mahogany furniture.

All fourteen members of the family lived here. All fourteen of them had assembled in this living room now. Harriet stood next to her three brothers. Everyone was hollering at one another, mostly in anguish and agreement.

In the center of the group was an old woman laying on a couch. She wore an oversized yellow t-shirt and jean shorts. Her eyes were closed and there was a bandage on the back of her head and around one wrist. Next to her sat a concerned medic, taking her blood pressure.

"I am going to kill that man," said Harriet, "whoever he is."

"He has attacked the matriarch and the grandson," said John Boy.

"That man must die," someone agreed.

"And this man says Bird Island has our stones," said William, nodding towards Cosmo.

"Maybe," corrected another.

"But it makes sense—"

"That family that live there, you don't want to mess with them—"

"It don't matter, they out here tryin to kill us—"

"It's their fight—"

A child brought around plastic cups of coconut water. Cosmo took one and studied Harriet's three brothers. Something about them looked different. Then he realized what it was.

They all had two different colored eyes. One blue and one brown, just like their sister. Evidently the gene ran in the family. He hadn't been able to see their eyes in the dark beach the previous night.

When he sensed a pause in the conversation, Cosmo said, "Can I offer another thought?"

The family turned to him. He carried some weight here, after all his efforts. They were willing to listen.

"I think you should go to Bird Island using a different tactic," he said.

"You saying violence isn't necessary," someone said.

"I'm saying save violence for the moment when it becomes necessary," Cosmo replied. "But there are other ways to approach this."

A woman said, "Like what? Pick up the phone? Everybody knows they are not that kind of people."

Cosmo remained diplomatically silent. He didn't want to suggest anything. He wanted the family to figure it out.

"We could concoct some kind of trick," said William.

Cosmo pointed at him. "There you go."

"But what kind of trick?" said another. "We hire a traveling salesman?"

Cosmo noticed Harriet looking at him with intensity.

"Tourists," she said.

He grinned. "I was waiting for someone to say that."

Harriet turned to her family and spoke. "I know how. William, we take your fishing boat. We bring a small group of tourists. Pretend they're on an ocean excursion. That's how we arrive at Bird Island."

John Boy nodded vigorously. "And we say we doin' a private tour, the port authorities don't ask questions why we going out at night."

The family grew quiet. This was plausible.

"But who do we use for tourists?" someone said.

The family turned to Cosmo. He pointed to his own sternum.

"Me?" he said. "Yeah, I can do it."

"But we need more than just you," said William. "Do you know anybody else who looks like a tourist?"

"He means white people," someone added.

The room laughed nervously at that. Cosmo nodded. "Oh yeah. Everybody at my conference. But it ends tomorrow night. They'll be leaving by then."

"So if we do this, we have to do it tonight," said Harriet.

"Right now," said William.

The Samaroo family all exchanged glances.

Two o'clock am.

The taxi van door slid open, and Robert Canavan spilled out onto the concrete, a plastic cup in his hand.

Cosmo helped him to his feet. Jones and LaRusso fell out a moment later, then picked themselves up. They were all halfway drunk, having spent the last few hours at the Terrace Bar.

Before them, the downtown docks awaited. Canavan wobbled in his sneakers, admiring the ships bobbing in the cool dark air. "So a nighttime cruise," he said.

"A private one," said Cosmo.

"How'd you find out about this?" said Jones.

Cosmo played it off. "I have my ways."

He guided all three of them down the pier towards the fishing vessel. The innocent lies flowed free and easy from his mouth. "So here's what they tell me. We have three stops. First, we'll look for the famous nightsharks. Second, we find the bioluminescent patch. Finally we make landing on Bird Island in time for the sunrise."

"This sounds great," said Canavan. "I've always wanted some adventure on the high seas."

They stopped in front of the fishing vessel. It was a trawler that had seen better days. The masthead light had been duct taped together, and the gantry looked like it'd been built out of spare parts. An inflatable orange dinghy sat on the rear of the boat. Patches of rust spotted the bow.

"This is a fishing boat," LaRusso said.

"That's what keeps their prices down," said Cosmo. "They do these tours on off nights, mostly for extra money."

Jones was studying him. "Something's up with you, Bennett."

"You know what's up? Four men on a party boat."

Canavan finished his drink, tottering on his heels, and tossed the plastic cup aside. "Bennett, don't you have to deliver a presentation tomorrow?"

"Not until two pm," he replied. "We'll be back by eight am. There's plenty of time."

He helped the three professors cross the plank and enter the boat. Onboard, four members of the Samaroo family waited for them.

The oldest man stuck out his hand. He wore a yacht captain's hat, the type with the short black brim and gold piping. The heavy sack of his belly pushed through his polo shirt.

"I'm Captain William," he said, "and welcome to my classic night tour of the eastern Caribbean. This is my nephew, Samuel."

The fit younger man shook their hands. He was wearing black neoprene wetsuit shorts and a loose white sleeveless t-shirt. On his feet were a pair of turquoise aqua shoes.

William gestured at the two other men securing loose equipment near the bow. "Over there is my crew, John Boy and George Jr. They're also my brothers."

Canavan clapped the man on his shoulder. "I have a very important question, Captain William."

"Yes sir."

"Where do you keep the beer?"

The captain laughed. "I have sixteen bottles waiting for you below deck in the freezer."

"Excellent," said Canavan.

"In Tatuaga we like to show people a good time. Please sit down, and we'll bring them out to you after departure."

It was a mercifully calm night. The trawler cruised over the gentle waves at a steady speed of thirteen knots. In the tiny bridge, Cosmo stood rubbing shoulders with William and Samuel.

"Your boys appear happy," said the captain.

Cosmo looked outside the window. Down below, Jones and LaRusso were clinking beer bottles at the front deck. Ahead of them, Canavan was peeing off the bow of ship with his arms outstretched in a wretched imitation of Jack and Rose.

"They're professors," he said.

"I wouldn't have guessed that," said Samuel.

"It's good they're so relaxed," said William, "because things are guaranteed to get tense on Bird Island."

"Let's go over the plan again," said Cosmo.

"We pretend the ship broke down. We take the dinghy to shore, find out what's happening, see what we can learn. We stay peaceful, no matter what."

"No matter what?" said Cosmo.

"That is the plan," said Samuel.

William leaned over and lowered his voice. "Plans do change, Dr. Bennett." Then he stood up straight again. "It's time. Go outside and tell them we couldn't find the nightsharks on the radar."

Cosmo went outside and down to the foredeck.

"Aaay," said LaRusso, "where's the beer?"

"It's flowing like molasses around here!" said Jones.

"Fellas, a bit of bad news. Captain William tells me that the nightsharks aren't coming up on radar."

"That sucks," said Canavan, zipping up his pants.

"What exactly is a nightshark anyways?" said LaRusso.

Cosmo lifted his palms and delivered his rehearsed explanation. "They said it was like an electrostatic fish or something. It only glows in the few hours before sunrise. I don't know. Anyways, we can't find them, so we're going directly to the bioluminescent patch."

"Give me more beer," said Canavan, "and I won't care where we go."

Half hour later, the trawler decelerated to a slow crawl over the dark water. "This is it," said Samuel. "The bioluminescent patch."

"I don't see anything," said Jones.

"Everybody return to the stern of the boat," said William, jerking a thumb over his shoulder. "It will be easier to see off the back."

Canavan, Jones, and LaRusso stumbled to the back of the trawler. They were laughing and giggling like children. Cosmo hoped it would continue that way.

The moment they had vacated the front deck, William nodded to his brothers. George Jr. and John Boy walked up to the bow and unscrewed several small bottles of powder and dumped them into the water.

"There it is," shouted Samuel, "I see the lights."

He was pointing off the back of the boat. Several large coils of luminescent water were glowing like writhing snakes in the water.

"What is it?" said Canavan.

"Nobody can explain it," said Samuel. "Not even top scientists. It's very famous."

Cosmo sidled up to John Boy. "What did you dump in the water?" he whispered.

John Boy whispered back, "Sodium perborate." He handed Cosmo the bottle. The label read Instant Light Powder. "We been tricking the tourists with this for years. Government says we not supposed to do it anymore."

A few minutes later, Captain William stepped out onto aft deck. "Still awake, my friends? Everything good?"

The three professors were leaning over the railing, staring rapt at the water, searching for the coils of lighted water.

Jones gave a thumbs up.

"It's beautiful," LaRusso said.

"All right," said William, "whenever you're ready to go to Bird Island, just say the word."

Canavan turned around, suddenly serious. He pushed his glasses up with an index finger.

"I'm ready," he said.

FIFTEEN

BIRD ISLAND, EASTERN ANTILLES, CARIBBEAN

Forty minutes later, a pink glow had appeared above the eastern rim of the ocean. William downshifted the trawler to a slow crawl.

"There it is," he said.

Ahead, against the western darkness, a slim bit of rock appeared like an outgrowth from the ocean.

Bird Island.

The captain motored the vessel up to two hundred meters from the coast. Then he shut off the engine. John Boy threw an anchor into the water. The anchor winch spun madly, then stopped.

George Jr. looked at the winch. "Eighteen meters," he said.

Cosmo squinted, trying to get a better sightline on the island. It really was small, maybe three hundred meters across. The close end was very low elevation, nearly sea level, while the far end was a several meters higher. There, a steep cliff tumbled down to the water's edge. A sheet of rock covered the entire island—not one tree, bush, or plant in sight.

Cosmo noted two signs of human habitation. One was a brand-new silver aluminum pier, with concrete pilings painted bright red. The structure jutted fifty meters out into a natural cove formed by the shape of the island. It was there to accommodate the enormous yacht that was moored at the end of it. The thing was a beauty, twice as long as the trawler, not a speck of dirt, its sheer sides gleaming white even in the pre-dawn dimness.

On the rear was printed the name.

Diamonds Are Forever.

The other sign of humanity was a single house that had been constructed on the far end. Cosmo strained to see it from this distance. It appeared to be formed by hunks of limestone cemented together. It seemed that they'd quarried it from the island itself. The overall effect was of a striking but ugly rock goblin rising out of the island.

"Gentlemen, here it is," said Captain William.

Canavan, Jones, and LaRusso stood on deck, arms crossed. They seemed vaguely bored, likely because they were sobering up.

"So what's to do here?" Canavan said.

"We go ashore and explore. There's nothing like it anywhere in the Caribbean," said William.

"There seems to be someone living there," Canvan said.

"Them don't bother nobody," said William. "Come on —we gonna have coffee and pastry once we get there."

"Now you've got me moving," said LaRusso, standing up.

"I'm game," said Jones.

Cosmo slung his backpack over his shoulders as John Boy and George Jr. attached the gantry hook to the dinghy ring strap. At the control, Samuel threw the shifter forward, hoisting the small craft into the air. Then he swung the arm to the right and threw the control downward. It slowly lowered the dinghy into the ocean, hitting the water with a gentle thump. Using a telescoped hook-pole, John Boy and George Jr pulled the dinghy beneath the railing hatch and tied it to a cleat onboard the trawler.

John Boy leapt into the small boat and started up the outboard engine. On his signal, Cosmo and the three professors descended a short ladder into the dinghy and seated themselves on the inflatable benches. William followed afterwards, carrying a red duffle bag. Finally, George Jr. entered the boat.

Onboard the trawler, Samuel untied the rope from the cleat.

"Are you coming?" said Canavan.

"No," Samuel replied, "I'm staying here to watch the boat. Have a good time."

Canavan's eyes roved down to the nephew's neoprene wetsuit pants. In his hand were a pair of swim goggles.

"Whatever you say," muttered the professor.

John Boy turned his wrist. The motor responded, and the dinghy lurched forward. He turned the rudder and circled the small boat towards the island.

As they pitched on the waves, William turned to the three professors, raising his voice to be heard over the motor and the wind. "If it's okay with you, let us handle all the talking."

"So they're not friendly," said LaRusso.

"Yes and no."

"But they welcome visitors?" asked Canavan.

The captain searched for a good explanation. "It's hard to explain. You'll see."

The ride was brief. Two minutes later, they were tying up to the pier in the shadow of the white yacht.

"Someone's not doing too badly here," muttered LaRusso, peering up at the side of the vessel.

Cosmo clambered up the ladder to the pier first, and Jones and LaRusso followed with minor difficulty. But Canavan froze on the rungs, clinging to the ladder.

"Come on," said Jones, "you got this."

"I'm just not good at these things," he said.

"You have to trust yourself."

"It's only four rungs," LaRusso added.

Canavan lifted his left leg to the second one. His face was squinched tightly in agony.

"Go on," said Cosmo.

The professor slowly pulled his upper body up until his right leg, scrambling, found the rung.

"I really hate this," he said.

"You can do it," Jones said again, "come on!"

A minute later, Canavan finally hauled himself onto the pier. The portly professor lay there on his back, breathing hard, his shirt riding up over his flabby middle section.

"I'm not an adventurer," he said, between gasps. "I sit at a desk. I talk at a podium. This is what I do. I've been doing it for thirty years."

"You can make yourself whatever you want to be," said Cosmo.

He sat up and looked at Cosmo. "Can I? Is that really true, Dr. Bennett?"

Cosmo nodded. "I believe it is."

Then Cosmo looked back at the trawler. In the distance, he saw the figure of Samuel dive into the water, long knife in hand, and begin swimming.

The group of seven walked single file down the pier to the island. A small tool shed made of cemented rocks greeted them.

"Let's see what's inside," said Jones.

"Maybe let's wait—" said Canavan.

Too late. Jones had yanked the metal door open. Inside was a riot of deep-sea fishing gear. Racks of rods, spools of nylon line, boxes of tackle, messes of nets, stacks of buckets.

"That's a serious cache," LaRusso said.

The professors moved on. William caught George Jr. by the sleeve.

"Cut them," he whispered.

George Jr. nodded. He produced a knife from his pocket, stepped into the shed, and slashed the lines and nets.

The group crossed the small rocky plain. It felt like walking across the surface of the moon.

"Limestone karst," said LaRusso, kicking a rock.

"It abounds in the Caribbean," Jones said.

"You two are talking like a couple of geographers or something," said Canavan.

"Crazy, isn't it?" said LaRusso.

"I mean, technically you're cartographers."

Jones made two circles with his thumbs and middle fingers. Then he brought them together so they were totally overlapping. "Venn diagram of my work and a geographer's work."

Canavan grinned. "Not fair, your specialization is topography—"

"We can't all be interested in gerrymandering, Robert."

Leaving the joshing behind, Cosmo ran ahead of the

other three professors and alongside William. "You see the name of that yacht?"

"It was the first thing I noticed," said William, his face set tight and serious. "I noticed something else too."

"What's that?"

"Bird Island don't have any birds."

Cosmo looked around. He was right. The rocks were empty of all animals, including winged ones. That could mean anything, including the idea that his hypothesis about the diamonds was correct. But he felt that this family was less interested in half-century-old gemstones than they were in revenge.

"You heard me ask your friends not to speak when we meet the people," William said. "That includes you, Dr. Bennett."

"Okay"

"You've helped us so much, I mean that. But this no longer concerns you. It's a family matter now."

"I'm just a tourist," Cosmo said.

"That's right," said William. "You play your part, and let us play ours."

"Boss," said John Boy. He was pointing ahead.

Someone was walked towards them across the island.

CHAPTER
SIXTEEN

The three brothers stopped in their tracks. All three reached behind their backs, where Cosmo noticed they carried sheathed knives. The breeze carried the brackish smell of saltwater and tidepools into his nostrils.

"Caution," said William. "Play the roles, and do not escalate."

The three professors caught up to them. "What's going on?" said Canavan.

Cosmo pointed ahead. "The local is here."

The figure drew nearer. The wind was rising along with the sun, so that everybody's hair blew sideways. Cosmo studied the man as he approached. He was short and stocky, his ochre skin reflecting the sun. A full nest of curly hair sprouted from his head. He wore a long-sleeved blue t-shirt and a pair of gray board shorts. His bare feet were splayed arrogantly wide apart and he stood on the rough rocky surface like a mixed martial arts challenger. A pair of wraparound sunglasses were on his face. A knife hung loosely in his right hand.

He came within vocal distance, then stopped.

"Morning," shouted William.

"What you do here?" the man replied. He had a high-pitched voice. His lips and nose had drawn tightly together for protection.

"We were conducting a night boat tour for these tourists," said William, "and we had some engine problems. Your island was the closest land we could find."

"We had engine problems?" whispered LaRusso.

"The engine worked fine," Jones whispered back.

Cosmo shushed them with a finger to his lips.

"What you want?" the man said.

"Some help with repairs," said William.

"We don't help."

"What do you people do?"

"Fish."

Canavan pointed towards the yacht. "I don't think fishing bought that."

"Shouldn't he be used to visitors asking for help?" said Jones.

"This feels wrong," added LaRusso.

Cosmo went over to Jones and LaRusso and guided them away from the scene. "I don't think you're really helping resolve anything."

Canavan backed away too. "LaRusso's right. Something is wrong here, Bennett."

The Bird Island resident lifted his knife and slapped it lightly against his palm. His eyes studied the three family members. "You're from Tatuaga."

"That's right."

His eyes narrowed even more, until they were barely visible slits.

"You go now," he said. The knife slapped the palm again.

"We're just a tourist expedition," said William. "We need help."

The man shook his head no, then pointed the knife back toward the pier.

William exchanged looks with George Jr. and John Boy. It was time. They nodded.

All three reached behind them and withdrew their own knives.

"Oh shit," said Jones, taking another few steps backwards.

LaRusso ran a nervous hand through his hair. "Cosmo, I feel like you should've mentioned this was a possible scenario, at some point."

Cosmo stayed a few short steps behind the three brothers. His fists clenched. His feet bounced nervously.

"I want the man who sliced my nephew," said William, his voice cracking with anger. "The boy goes by Desmond. He said it was a big man did it. Drew his knife across Desmond's chest in Tatuaga five days ago." He illustrated by drawing his own index finger across his chest.

The game had changed. Now the truth was out in the open, flopping and gasping like a fish on the deck of a boat.

Cosmo looked at the other professors. Canavan was staring back at him with a mixture of loathing and surprise.

"You knew about this, Bennett," he said. "This was all a setup."

Cosmo searched for words. There weren't any. He was guilty.

"I never said I was perfect," he finally replied.

The man from Bird Island turned his head and whooped. It was a strange sound. It felt like it came from a foreign species.

Less than a hundred meters away, the front door opened on the rock-goblin house. Two figures stepped out.

A man and a woman.

Both were huge. The man was bald and mean and looked like a double-wide refrigerator with shoes. The woman was nearly as big, with an angry face and a long black ponytail. Both wore wraparound sunglasses.

"Bulge dey gwinne give pain," the man shouted.

"That's him," said William, pointing at Bulge. "That's the big man. Desmond said it."

It happened so fast that Cosmo nearly missed it. In a flash, William, John Boy, and George Jr. were upon the man closest to them. The man's knife slashed at the air, but the three brothers quickly surrounded and subdued him. John Boy grabbed his wrist and wrenched the knife from his hand. George put him in a half-nelson. And William held him by his hair and jammed his knee into the man's face.

Bulge began running towards them across the rocks. So did the female.

Cosmo turned backwards. Two of the professors, Jones and LaRusso, were running as fast as they could across the rocks, back towards the dinghy.

But not Canavan. He was watching the action, transfixed.

"Go!" shouted Cosmo.

The professor didn't move. He was frozen in place.

"Bennett," shouted William, one hand still holding the man's hair, "get the ties from my bag!"

Cosmo scrambled over to the red duffle bag. He unzipped it and found a pack of plastic ties. He tossed one to William, who caught it with his free hand. He handed it to John Boy, who circled it around the man's wrists and cinched it tight.

They dropped the man on the rocks, now bleeding from his nose and bound at the wrists. The trio turned to face the wall of flesh hurtling towards them across the landscape.

The man they called Bulge wasted no time in identifying his target. It was William. He headed directly for the oldest brother, who fell back onto his rear foot and prepared his knife arm. But William wasn't young and was slow to react. Bulge had guessed this, and sped up as he drew closer.

In a half second, Bulge was upon the older captain, running over him like a hippopotamus stampeding its prey.

Cosmo backpedaled several meters, standing next to Canavan.

"What do we do?" said Canavan.

"They told me not to get involved."

Within seconds, the conflict had become an all-out melee. Bulge was swinging his massive fists wildly, with John Boy circling him, jabbing where he could with the knife. Meanwhile, the woman had put George Jr. in a headlock. He was twisting hard, but her flex was strong, and she had already begun pulling him across the rocks.

William still lay on the ground. "Bennett!" he shouted.

"Okay, time to get involved," Cosmo said.

He took a deep breath, picked up a fist-sized rock, and ran up behind Bulge. Up close, Cosmo guessed that the man was at least twice his own weight. The only reason anybody could stand a chance against him was the fact that it was an open-air fight with plenty of room to maneuver. In a closed room, he'd destroy all comers.

Cosmo hauled back and threw the rock as hard as he could into the center of the man's massive back. The giant threw his arms in the air and staggered forward a step. John Boy saw his chance and came at the giant once more, but Bulge shoved him across the rocks by the face. John

Boy stumbled backwards, arms windmilling, and landed on his back. His eyes flew open. He rolled over, clearly in pain.

It was a sharp rock, right under the point where his lower back had landed.

John Boy, out.

Crap.

Bulge slowly turned around. Cosmo felt his knees go weak with fear. He'd done some boxing training years earlier, so he remembered the techniques, had some muscle memory. But he'd hadn't been in a real fight in a while, and certainly never against anyone like this.

But Cosmo was smart. He sussed out the only possible strategy.

Tire out the big man.

Bulge's first swing came from the left. It was quick, but Cosmo ducked. He heard it whistle in the air over his head. Deciding not to counterattack, Cosmo instead circled around the opposite way, towards Bulge's rear. The giant swiveled quickly—he was surprisingly fast for a half-ton of muscle and fat—and sent another jab towards Cosmo's head. This one was stronger than the last, coming from the center of the giant's body, but Cosmo leaned right a half-second before it arrived. He felt the punch sizzle near his ear.

He bobbed down, crabwalked left, and popped up on the opposite side from where Bulge would've expected. Annoyed, the giant turned his head, saw him, and swung a quick backhand. The blow connected across Cosmo's clavicle and sent him staggering backwards a few steps. Disoriented, he struggled to find his footing. This was enough time for Bulge to turn around, close the gap between them, and grab Cosmo by the shirt.

"Canavan!" shouted Cosmo. "I need help!"

Trembling, Robert Canavan timidly picked his way across the rocks. "Yes, yes, coming—"

Bulge hauled smacked Cosmo with his open right hand. Cosmo's teeth rattled in his skull and his face went numb. Bulge smacked him again, harder, and the world went black for a brief moment. Cosmo came back to his senses and tried to shake it off. It wouldn't shake off.

"Robert!" he said.

Through the blur, Cosmo saw the outline of the professor gingerly picking his way over to John Boy. He saw the professor take the knife from his hand.

"Thank you, sir," said Canavan, "I will return this shortly."

Meanwhile, Bulge still held Cosmo by the shirt with his left hand. With his right, he hauled back and sent a single punch square into Cosmo's gut.

Cosmo gasped and went cross-eyed. It felt like being disemboweled. And he knew that was only a fraction of what Bulge was capable of.

Canavan minced his way over to Bulge's back, a look of consternation on his face. The giant had his back to the professor. Canavan took a deep inhale.

The giant heard him, began to turn—

"Do it," said Cosmo.

Robert Canavan, lifelong professor of cartography, hesitated for a split moment. Then he stuck the four-inch blade into Bulge's back, on the left side, just below the shoulder blade. It went in smooth, like a butter knife into a bowl of frosting.

"Oh, that was easy," he said.

Bulge dropped Cosmo onto the rocks. He whirled. Cocked his arm back.

And punched Canavan directly in the face. With full strength.

A line of blood arced out of his nose and spattered the air. A second later, the professor was flat on his back, on the ground.

Bulge returned his attention to Cosmo, a knife sticking out of his back. His face was enraged. He lifted both arms into the air, preparing to grab his helpless prey on the ground.

But Cosmo had reached over his own shoulder, and into his open backpack. There, he'd found a good friend.

Chester.

With a single slash, Cosmo ran the machete across the giant's chest, from left to right. A sheet of blood instantly appeared and began to trickle down his torso.

Bulge looked down in shock. "What you do that for?"

Cosmo, still on the ground, couldn't believe the question. "Self-defense, you donkey."

But Bulge still didn't fall. He looked more confused than anything.

William had dragged himself to his feet. Now he appeared at Cosmo's side. "Give me that," he said.

He unpeeled Cosmo's fingers from the handle of the machete. He stood in front of Bulge. "That was from my nephew. But this is from all the Samaroos."

The boat captain ran the machete into Bulge's chest, between the ribs, straight into the heart.

The giant's face went white. His eyeballs rolled upwards. And he began to topple forward.

Cosmo quickly rolled to the left. With a thud, the man they called Bulge hit the ground where Cosmo had been two seconds earlier. On the back of his neck, in a neat line from left to right, was a tattoo.

Diamants sont éternels.

William stood over the man's body. Cosmo joined him.

"What does that mean?" said William.

"Diamonds are forever," Cosmo replied.

They stood there, breathing for a moment.

Cosmo turned to the man. "It's been a lovely tour, William."

"It's not over yet, Dr. Bennett," the captain replied. "Look."

CHAPTER
SEVENTEEN

Ahead, Bulge's female counterpart was hauling George Jr. across the rocks towards the house. His heels were dragging on the rocks, his body limp, his eyes were closed.

She'd choked him out.

Cosmo went over to Canavan, helped him sit up. He wiped the blood off the professor's face.

"It's true, you really can become anything," the professor said. "I just made myself into a murderer."

"No," said Cosmo, "that was William. You made yourself into an assailant."

Canavan looked up at Cosmo. "Why the hell did you drag me out here? I could've been asleep in my room all night."

"We needed a cover, and you said wanted some adventure," answered Cosmo. "Now you have a great story."

Canavan held up a single warning finger. Then he gently slapped Cosmo in the cheek.

"That's for being a dick," he said.

"I deserve it," Cosmo said. Then he peered at Canavan's face. "I think your nose is broken, Robert. Use this—and stay here."

Cosmo handed him a towel from the duffle bag. Then he picked his way across the rocks to where John Boy and William were limping towards the house, knives hanging from their hands.

Up ahead, the hefty woman had pulled herself and the unconscious George Jr. up against the wall of the rock-goblin house. She held a knife to his throat.

"Cat foot soft but he does scratch hard!" she shouted.

That didn't make a lot of sense, but it didn't matter. To Cosmo, that was a threat in any dialect. The context was the knife against the throat.

"Moon ah run til daylight ketch am," William shouted back.

Cosmo didn't know what that meant either. He wasn't exactly up to speed on his Guyanese slang. But it must've been insulting because the woman spat on the ground in response. Then she pushed the blade harder against the unconscious man's neck.

They were in a hostage situation. Cosmo edged over towards the pair. "What should we do?"

John Boy was unsuccessfully trying to contain a grin.

"Why are you smiling?" said Cosmo.

William answered from the side of his mouth. "Just wait."

Cosmo turned and waited. Soon a movement caught his eye. On the roof of the rock-goblin house came a stealthy figure, crawling low, knife in his teeth. He wore a pair of black neoprene wetsuit shorts and a pair of turquoise aqua shoes.

It was Samuel.

"Keep her talking," Cosmo said, "so Samuel can hear her position."

William cupped his hands around his mouth. "Yuh diggin hole to fill hole," he shouted.

"Nah," she replied.

The fit man in the neoprene shorts drew up to the very edge of the roof. He peered down at the woman and her hostage.

"What hurts eye does mek node wateh," shouted John Boy.

"So you say," she replied, "but that not how it go."

In one swift movement, Samuel leapt from the roof onto the ground next to the woman. Startled, she instinctively slashed at him, but he pulled himself away as the blade whistled past his midsection. Quickly, he kicked it out of her hand with his left foot. The knife clattered on the rocks a short distance away.

"Now," said William.

The three of them dashed up to the house. They were on her in an instant, all four men, but the large woman was thrashing like a killer whale. John Boy and Samuel succeeded in pinning down her two arms. Cosmo tried to grab her legs, but she kicked him off. He went to George Jr. instead and helped him sit up.

William stood over her and pressed his foot into her throat. He switched back to standard English. "We know about the birds. We know about the mine. This man here showed us."

He nodded to Cosmo. The woman's eyes went to him.

"Now tell us everything else."

She spat at him.

"George Jr wants to help you remember," he said.

George Jr. was on his feet now. He kicked her lightly in the head, as if that would jog her memory.

"Tell us the story," William ordered.

"Nah."

William nodded to his brother. George Jr. kicked her again, but harder this time.

"Tell us."

The woman tilted her head back and screamed at the top of her lungs. It was a loud but eerie sound, like an anguished gargle. Then she hocked another piece of saliva at William.

"Somebody bring my bag," he said.

Cosmo turned. Further back, near the body of the giant, Canavan had risen to his feet and was cleaning his glasses.

"The bag!" he shouted, motioning to bring it.

Canavan dutifully picked up the duffle bag and shuffled towards the rock-goblin house. When he arrived, William reached inside and found a roll of duct tape. He ripped off a piece and bent down and taped the woman's mouth shut.

"Thank you for the help," he said.

"Boss," said Samuel. He was standing in the doorway of the house, pointing inside. "There's somebody else here."

William regarded the woman on the ground. "Let's tie her up and we go in."

John Boy and George Jr. rolled the woman onto her side, her muffled screams sounding beneath the duct tape. They pinned her arms behind her. William crouched down and snapped the plastic tie onto her wrists.

"Don't go anywhere," he said.

They stood up. George Jr. kicked her once more in the head, a bit too savagely. It dislodged her wraparound sunglasses.

Cosmo crouched down and pulled them fully off her face. She opened her eyes and looked at him with hatred.

He sucked in his breath.

The woman's eyes were two different colors.

Blue and brown.

Cosmo stood up and followed the three brothers into the rock-house. He didn't say anything about what he'd discovered.

Whereas the exterior of the house was crude and primitive, the interior couldn't have been more different. It took Cosmo a moment to adjust.

He found himself in a slick and modern design. The open kitchen boasted spotless white countertops, brand-new sink, and cool finishes. In the living room, a red modular Italian sofa looked out through the sliding glass door onto the ocean. It looked like part of a contemporary design catalog. In the corridor, intricate crystal structures had been placed in hand-hewn rock alcoves.

Cosmo soaked in the ambience. "This feels like a Bond villain's lair."

"Where is the other person, Samuel?" said William.

His nephew pointed to a bedroom. The door was partly open.

"We safe?"

"It's an old one," said Samuel.

Cosmo and William stepped into the bedroom. It was a simple room, with a row of black-and-white photos on an aged dresser. A window at the far end admitted the morning light. The queen bed in the middle of the room was nearly immaculate—except for one thing.

A withered elderly man was laying tucked in the bed, the immaculate white sheets pulled up to his ribcage. His arms lay peacefully on either side of his body.

Cosmo studied his face. The old man's mouth was open in a perpetual gasp, and his lips seemed to have curled around and disappeared behind his teeth. His short hair was entirely white. His eyelids were closed.

"Is he alive?" said Cosmo.

"Sir," said William.

The old man's eyes slowly opened. He turned his head and looked at the visitors. Cosmo noticed that both the man's eyes were brown.

"What is this?" The voice came out like a croak.

William stowed away his knife. "I'm William Samaroo, from Tatuaga. I'm the son of George Samaroo. These are his other sons. We come to find you."

The man's face darkened. "I don't like Tatuaga. My family don't like it."

"We know."

The man lost himself in thought for a moment. Cosmo watched his face travel through a journey of emotions— recollection, anger, acceptance.

Finally, he came back to the present. "How is George doing?"

"George is passed on," said William. "Three months ago."

"Oh."

The old man said it again to himself. "George Samaroo is dead." His body seemed to deflate a little.

"You knew him well?"

"Aye."

"You smuggled diamonds out of Guyana with him."

The old man slowly nodded. "I did."

CHAPTER
EIGHTEEN

There it was. The full confession. Certain elderly people were easy to hoodwink because they forget to think before they speak. Whatever flies out of their mouths surprises them just as much as it does their listeners.

"And you cheated him out of his portion of the diamonds?" said William.

Cosmo's eyes widened in surprise. William wasted no time in getting to the point.

The elderly man grew angry. Full of new fire, he tried to pull himself up in bed. "Who are you come in my house and say that?"

"William Samaroo, son of George Samaroo—"

"Those stones were half mine! I trained the birds. They followed me in my plane. I flew the plane—more than one hundred times! I paid for the fuel. You tell George that!"

"George Samaroo is dead," William reminded him.

"Did our father raise the birds?" John Boy asked the old man.

"We did it together," the old man said, calming down.

"I trained them to follow me in my plane. He took them into the mine."

"How many diamonds did you get out?"

The old man was fully awake now. "Hundreds. We lost a few birds but most of them made it here. We listed the weight in the corner of the maps."

Cosmo remembered the mysterious decimals in the corners of the maps. Those were the carat measurements.

"You said the stones were half his. You split everything fifty-fifty with our father?"

The old man pulled himself up to a sitting position. "I was fair to George until he done what he done."

The pause lingered in the room like a bad smell. The three brothers looked at one another. Cosmo could barely breath from the pressure.

"What our father done?" said George Jr.

"You know what he done," came the reply.

"No, we don't," said William.

The old man crossed his arms. Looked away.

"So you don't speak anymore now?"

The old man said, "Tatiana! Tati!"

"Your daughter isn't coming. Neither are the two boys."

Cosmo decided to intervene. He stepped between William and the old man and faced the three Samaroo brothers. "Before this goes any further, I have to show you something."

"Right now?" said William.

"Yes, right now." He looked at the others. "All of you. Come outside with me."

Cosmo pointed to the door. The three brothers, plus Samuel, went out into the corridor and left the rock-goblin house.

Outside, Cosmo saw Canavan standing next to the

woman, Tatiana. She had struggled to her knees and was breathing hard, her hair in her face.

"Oh thank God you're here," said the professor. "Every time she gets to her feet, I have to kick her over again."

Cosmo headed over to the woman, the Samaroo family following. He walked up to her, motioning for the family to draw closer. They did. She began screaming beneath the duct tape, but he ignored it.

"Robert, could you hold her head still?"

Canavan grimaced. He went behind the woman and held her skull with both hands.

Cosmo got down on his knees. "Tatiana, we're not going to hurt you. Just open your eyes for me."

She kept her eyes clenched. Frustrated, Cosmo changed tactics. Using the index finger and thumb of each hand, he forced her eyelids open.

"Look at her eyes," he said to the brothers.

The brothers stooped down. All three of them suddenly leaped back.

"She's like us!" said George Jr.

"Maybe she is one of us," said John Boy.

"Let's look at the other two," said William. "I bet they're all related."

Cosmo followed the Samaroo family as they ran down the island, back to where they'd dropped the first brother. He'd pulled himself to a cross-legged position. They pulled off his wraparound sunglasses and pried open his eyes.

Blue and brown.

They were stunned. "Who wants to check the big man?" said Samuel.

"I will," said William.

They walked over to Bulge's corpse. His head had turned to the side when he fell. William bent down and opened his eyes. Then he straightened up and nodded.

"What is going on here?" said Samuel.

"There's one person who has that answer," Cosmo said, pointing back to the rock-goblin house. The old man was now standing in the doorway, leaning on his walker. Cosmo guessed that his eyesight was poor enough that he couldn't see that Bulge had been killed.

They walked briskly back to the man.

"Why all them have different eyes?" said William.

"It's our gift," he said.

"You know our family has different eyes too?"

The old man didn't twitch. Didn't blink. But something told Cosmo that he had heard every word.

"Those are George's children," the elderly man said.

Plain and simple. Flat and factual.

"No, those are your children," said William.

"No, they're not. They're family to you."

The three brothers drew closer together. Samuel edged away, closer to Cosmo.

"Who was the mother?" said William.

"My wife."

The cold fire that came into the old man's eyes made it clear that he wasn't lying. "She was going to Tatuaga every month or two to sell another group of diamonds. She had to do it because they started recognizing me at the shops. She got with your father on those trips."

"Where is she now?"

"Dead."

"How?"

"She fell from a cliff. Long time ago."

"On Tatuaga," said William. "I remember that. I was a very young man. The authorities never figured out how it happened."

The old man stayed silent. His fingers gripped the walker more tightly.

The three brothers turned around. Two people tied and bound on the ground. One more, dead.

Family.

"What about the diamonds?" said William.

"They long gone," replied the old man. "We sold the last ones fourteen, fifteen years ago. Went all over the region to do it."

Cosmo nodded. That explained the yacht.

"You kept our share of the diamonds because your wife gave you the horns," said John Boy.

"With our father," said George Jr.

The old man said nothing. He wasn't sorry. He wasn't anything at all. It was a historical fact now, a fossil of the distant past that couldn't be changed.

"That big one," said John Boy, "what was his name?"

"His name is John," came the old man's reply.

"He tried to kill one of ours. To get the maps of the migrations that George left us."

"Unfortunate."

"That man is dead now. Right over there."

The old man peered over their shoulders towards Bulge's body. "My boy."

"He tried to kill my mother."

"He was your blood."

There didn't seem to be anything to say to that. Cosmo got the feeling that things were about to get really weird. He quietly approached William. "I have to leave now."

The eldest Samaroo brother nodded. "Samuel can take you back. We gonna stay here."

"Okay," Cosmo said, "but I have to say one more thing."

"What," said William.

Cosmo leaned in. "There are still diamonds on this island."

William's eyes darted towards him. "How you know that?"

"Why else would that big man want the maps? To the point where he would attack your family?"

William rubbed his chin and thought. "We will turn this place upside down and find them."

"You do that."

Cosmo turned away and motioned to Canavan. "We're leaving now."

"What the hell is going on here, Bennett?" the professor said.

"I'll explain it all later," Cosmo replied. "Let's get back to the boat."

Cosmo, Canavan, and Samuel crossed the island to the pier. Jones and LaRusso were sitting in the dinghy.

"Still waiting on that pastry and coffee," said LaRusso.

"You got a special experience though," said Cosmo.

The men climbed into the dinghy. Samuel turned on the motor and pointed it back towards the trawler.

CHAPTER
NINETEEN

THE ISLAND OF TATUAGA, EASTERN ANTILLES, CARIBBEAN

One fifty-five pm.

Cosmo ran a comb through his wet hair and checked his teeth in the mirror. They'd returned by ten am, and he'd lain down for what was supposed to be a short nap. He'd woken up twenty minutes before his scheduled speech.

He ran through the resort to the main ballroom, his open laptop in hand, staring at the screen.

"Come on, Noah, come on—"

His email inbox was depressingly full of messages he didn't care about. He only wanted one email.

There. It had just popped up, from Noah. The subject line: Updated Powerpoint.

He quickly hit download. Cosmo's feet shuffled across the carpet and bumped into several conference attendees. His eyes scanned the presentation.

"Yes," said Cosmo, "this is exactly what I needed." He made a chef's kiss.

In the ballroom, Canavan was waiting next to the stage. He wore a new shirt and pants and he looked surprisingly chipper. There was no sign of what they'd endured that morning, except for the white bandage that ran across the bridge of his nose.

"I don't even know where to begin with you," he said.

Cosmo nodded towards the microphone. "You could start with a quick introduction?"

He slung the backpack off his shoulder onto a table. The compartment was unzipped, and Chester the machete clattered out onto the table.

Several attendees sitting near the front gasped. Embarrassed, Cosmo smiled at them as he slipped the machete back into his pack. "That wasn't supposed to happen."

Canavan gave him a look that was a mixture of anger, admiration, and exasperation. "We're going to talk later, Dr. Bennett."

"I'd love to," said Cosmo.

Canavan put a hand on Cosmo's neck and gave him a hard squeeze. It was a good sign.

Then he climbed onstage, and Cosmo followed him.

PLOTWORKS
PUBLISHING

Visit Plotworks Publishing to follow Cosmo Bennett in *Boundary*, his first full-length mapping thriller!

Turn the page for a sneak peek—

J.A. JERNAY

BOUNDARY

A COSMO BENNETT MAPPING THRILLER

FROM THE AUTHOR OF THE AINSLEY WALKER
GEMSTONE TRAVEL MYSTERY SERIES

BOUNDARY

Cosmo and his assistant Noah shuffled down the dirt shoulder of the boulevard in the midday heat, sweating and miserable.

Each was lost in his own thoughts. Cosmo dreamed of hitting a heavy punching bag at his gymnasium. Noah dreamed of passing level nineteen of Operation Earlobe, an obscure RPG he'd abandoned last semester.

The morning's meeting had been a complete bust.

"I don't think we should continue," said Cosmo finally.

Noah didn't respond, but Cosmo took no notice. He continued: "I don't think anybody here takes our task seriously. I don't think this propaganda map was as influential as they say. I don't think this map has driven the civil unrest. I think social media and centuries of tribal warfare are more to blame for the unrest than anything else."

He looked over at Noah, waiting for a response. "What about you?"

The graduate assistant came back from his reverie. "Huh?"

"Did you hear anything I said?"

"No."

"I was just saying this is pointless and we should go home."

"I don't have a problem with that."

They arrived at Vida e Caffe. It was a chain café, with hundreds of similar franchises scattered across the southern half of the African continent. The branding was modern and inviting. A hundred people sat beneath umbrellas at small tables on the large outdoor patio.

An arm was waving at them. It was Christopher, their fixer, a cup of tea on a ceramic saucer in front of him. Two other cups awaited them.

"Hello sirs," he said. "I ordered us all a rooibos. It's a vanilla tea that is extraordinary."

Cosmo and Noah pulled out the chairs and sat down. The driver quickly sussed out that something was wrong.

"It was a bad meeting?" he said quietly.

"Yes," said Cosmo, "there was no progress made."

"I'm very sorry."

Cosmo sighed. "I think we have to leave."

The fixer looked confused. "But you just sat down—"

"The country," he clarified. "We have to leave Faba-jouti. We can't seem to do any good here."

Christopher looked crestfallen. "I do understand your frustration."

Noah said, "If it's okay with you, we'd probably like to just get in the car and go back to the hotel."

The fixer rediscovered his manners. "Of course, as you wish—"

"But we'd love to try the tea first—" added Cosmo.

"You two enjoy the rooibos," said Christopher, "while I fetch the car. The parking lot is very jammed and it will take quite a while to remove. I've already paid the bill."

Before they could object, the driver had shot to his feet. He clapped Cosmo on the shoulder and left the patio. They watched him cross the boulevard to an off-street parking area that was crammed tightly with vehicles. On his approach, the attendant began shifting other vehicles.

Noah sipped the tea. "This does taste really good. I don't drink enough tea."

"I like tea," said Cosmo. He sipped from the cup. "This one is good."

"What's your favorite?" asked Noah.

"Maybe pu'er."

"That one's bitter, right?"

"Yeah. It's fermented."

"What about Earl Grey?"

"A cliché."

"I think I'm more of a fruity tea guy," said Noah.

Cosmo nodded. "Yeah, they have their charms."

"You ever try chamomile?"

"It's good for sleeping," said Cosmo, "but otherwise it's—"

His comment was cut short by a massive fireball that erupted from the parking lot across the street.

In a split second, Cosmo and Noah instinctively rolled off their chairs and onto the ground beneath their table. Their eyes met. Each was filled with terror.

Then the shock of the overpressure hit. Cosmo felt the force of the blast wave hit the left side of his body. The highly compressed air rattled the left side of his skull. It even sent his lips and cheeks flapping to the right.

The initial sound of the explosion was deafening, but that was soon replaced by a symphony of falling destruction. A thousand pieces of metal, plastic, glass, and upholstery rained down upon the boulevard, the grass, the other cars.

A shower of tiny shrapnel hit on the patio of the cafe. One hit Noah in the hand and sizzled his flesh. He shook it off.

They waited another few seconds for the shrapnel rain to end. Then Cosmo and Noah lifted their heads.

The patio of the café was transformed into pandemonium. The patrons started to pull themselves up from the ground and flee out to the street and in the opposite direction. The street itself was coming alive with panicked people running in every direction.

"What the actual—" said Noah.

"Christopher!" interrupted Cosmo. "What about Christopher?"

He scrambled up to his feet. Without waiting for Noah, he sprinted out of the café and across the boulevard, weaving through the stopped cars. The air was acrid with chemicals and the heat had somehow intensified even further.

The parking lot was a field of wreckage. The bomb had exploded in the middle of the space, shredding every vehicle and person within twenty meters. Pieces of concrete and metal and glass had been blown across the scene.

"Christopher!" he shouted again. "Christopher! Don't do this!"

He saw a shoe with a foot still in it. He saw a red string of guts entangled in a hubcap. A wave of nausea gripped his stomach. He covered his nose with his t-shirt and backed away.

He tripped backwards over a piece of metal, stumbled, and fell to the ground.

That's when he saw it.

A long strip of shredded fabric. A yellow-and-green printed tropical shirt.

It was bloody and torn.

Cosmo turned his head and retched onto the asphalt. All the tea he'd just drank came out.

He somehow pulled himself to his feet and staggered back to the café. Noah was waiting at the far corner, on the sidewalk, pacing frantically.

"So?"

"I found him," said Cosmo. He forced the next words out. "A little bit."

Noah's face went white. "Oh my God."

Cosmo didn't say anything. He just gripped Noah by the upper arm. "Walk with me. And don't look back."

———

The pair moved briskly down the boulevard, away from the scene. People were running past them, mouths open, eyes full of fear, but Cosmo maintained a steady pace. His face betrayed an intense desire to appear as normal as possible.

"So we're just going to leave the scene?" said Noah.

"Yep."

"Why?"

"Don't make me answer that, Noah."

"I think we should talk to the police, cooperate, tell them everything—"

"In a different country," Cosmo replied, "in a different scenario, you'd be right. But not here, not now."

Noah looked back over his shoulder at the scene.

"Look straight ahead," Cosmo said through his teeth, "and listen to me. Our Mercedes is gone. Christopher is … gone."

"Shit—"

"And I'm going to suggest something else that could blow your mind."

"What?"

"It's possible that we were the intended target."

"That's insane."

"Is it?"

"How do you know?"

"I don't. But it's a possibility. Here's another one. It's possible that we are going to be used as scapegoats. We were the last people seen eating with Christopher. Do you want to be put in a Fabajouti jail on suspicion of a crime?"

They walked for another half minute in silence. Behind them, the chaos grew distant.

"Where are we going?" Noah said finally.

"Back to the hotel."

"And then?"

"We're leaving, like we planned."

"We're not going home, are we?" said Noah.

Cosmo's mouth grew hard and his jaw jutted out. He stared straight forward at an invisible point on the horizon. "No, we're not."

PLOTWORKS
PUBLISHING

Visit Plotworks Publishing to follow Cosmo Bennett in *Boundary*, his first full-length mapping thriller!

Then explore another series by J.A. Jernay—the Ainsley Walker Gemstone Travel Mysteries!

Turn the page for a sneak peek—

THE

URUGUAY AMETHYST

AN AINSLEY WALKER
GEMSTONE TRAVEL MYSTERY

J.A. JERNAY

THE URUGUAY AMETHYST

Ainsley pulled the backseat door closed. Her driver's eyes looked at her in the rearview mirror.

"Where can I take you?" Oswaldo asked in Spanish.

"Back to Tabarez," she said.

He nodded, and they pulled away from the curb. Ainsley studied him in the mirror. His jaw was set firmly. She decided to see what she could learn from him.

"Do you like working for Tabarez?" she said.

"Yes," he said. Nothing else.

Of course he wouldn't comment on his employer. She decided to stick to facts.

"Oswaldo, after lunch I will need you to help me take a very large package to this address." She handed him the paper with Bernabé's address. "Can you find this place?"

He read the address and nodded. Not a word. Ainsley was beginning to wonder if he was a bit simple.

The car was slicing down La Rambla, and Ainsley contented herself with staring out the window, at the blurring breakwall and at the choppy brown water of the delta. The sky was bright blue and the clouds puffy and white and a chill wind was blowing again.

It was mesmerizing. She wrapped her coat around herself more tightly and snuggled in.

Then she woke up to Oswaldo touching her knee. The vehicle had stopped. She was outside Tabarez's house.

Ainsley emerged from the vehicle and buttoned the top collar of her coat. "It's so cold here," she said.

Oswaldo didn't respond. Conversationally, there was no difference between her driver and a piece of drywall. She decided to just issue him orders instead. It would save both of them a lot of trouble.

"Stay here until I return."

He lit a cigarette and looked straight ahead.

Slinging her purse over her shoulder, Ainsley walked alone towards the house. Her stomach was twisting itself into anxious knots. Partly because of El Árbol Negro, partly because she was so hungry.

And nervous. She was about to enjoy homemade ñoquis in a private dining room with an extremely wealthy and attractive man who may or may not have refused to sleep with her, even after she'd thrown herself at him. Why did she have to black out on that night of all nights? And now he was going to sell her a famous amethyst after telling her its secret history.

This felt too good to be true.

The copper gate was rolled wide open. Ainsley cocked her head. That was strange, given the value of the contents inside the mansion.

She stepped through the open gate onto the driveway, then moved into the manicured yard. It made her heart sing again. She touched the bougainvillea, listened to the branches clacking in the breeze from the estuary.

Then she rang the front doorbell and waited. The slab of wood before her was exquisite. Spirals and whorls had been dug into its surface, like the enormous thumbprint of a criminal.

There was no response. That was weird. Heinrik was the epitome of the efficient manservant. He should've been there in a flash.

She rang the doorbell again, then turned and surveyed the landscaping. Water was trickling from some unseen fountain. She couldn't find it. An invisible bird sang crookedly from the branches of a tall ash. She couldn't find that either. A sinking feeling filled her stomach.

Had she been lied to? Had Tabarez cast her aside that quickly? Had he decided to keep El Árbol Negro? She'd heard the old cliché of how Latin people lived for the moment, but this expulsion was quicker than she'd expected. She felt anger sprouting from her back like a bouquet of hot orange flames.

Upset, she turned back to the door. If he wouldn't answer the door, she would invite herself inside. She gripped the doorknob and turned it. The slab of wood swung open easily, as though it weighed ten pounds instead of twenty times that much. Of course Tabarez had made sure that the hinges were well-oiled.

She entered the foyer and noticed a large object, wrapped in black plastic, resting immediately next to the door.

El Árbol Negro.

With her fingertips she traced its lovely branches beneath the plastic. So beautiful. She noticed a dolly sitting next to it. How thoughtful.

Remembering her host's orders, she kicked off her shoes, then crept around the edges of the carpet. The house was completely silent.

"José Ignacio?" she shouted. "Heinrik?"

Still no response. She crept up the stairs to the second

floor sitting room where she had last seen him, in his white robe, strumming his instrument.

As she rose to the landing, she caught her breath.

José Ignacio was still sitting on the sofa in the sumptuous second floor sala. The guitar was laying next to him. His head was tilted back, and his eyes were shut. A thin smile decorated his mouth.

Another thin smile, this one quite a bit redder, and eight inches across, decorated his throat.

José Ignacio Tabarez was not going to be dining with her this afternoon.

He was dead.

PLOTWORKS
PUBLISHING

Visit Plotworks Publishing today for all these titles—and more!